# THE FRIEND ZONE

## DELANEY DIAMOND

The Friend Zone by Delaney Diamond

Copyright © 2021, Delaney Diamond

Garden Avenue Press

Atlanta, Georgia

ISBN: 978-1-946302-48-9 (Ebook edition)

ISBN: 978-1-946302-50-2 (Paperback edition)

Cover photography: Jazmin Quaynor at instagram.com/jazminantoinette

Cover model: Jazmin Quaynor

This book is a work of fiction. All names, characters, locations, and incidents are products of the author's imagination, or have been used fictitiously. Any resemblance to actual persons living or dead, locales, or events is entirely coincidental. No part of this e-book may be reproduced or shared by any electronic or mechanical means, including but not limited to printing, file sharing, and e-mail, without prior written permission from Delaney Diamond.

www.delaneydiamond.com

# 1

"Throw it to me, Daddy!" Prince screamed, jumping up and down.

Omar pretended to search among the group of screaming little boys for the right receiver, stepped back, and then tossed the Nerf football underhand to his four-year-old son. Prince caught it against his chest and took off running with five boys and girls around the same age racing after him. When he crossed into the end zone, he spiked the ball in the cutest way and did his rendition of the Falcons' Dirty Bird dance.

"That's my boy!" Omar hollered. He raced over and swept up Prince in his arms, spinning them in a circle.

Giggling, Prince flung his little arms around his father's neck. Patting him on the butt, Omar placed him on the ground.

"Good job. All right, guys, I gotta get some work done. Miss Julianne is going to take over."

A series of disappointed moans went up from the group.

"I'll catch you all another day," Omar promised.

"See you later, Daddy!" Green eyes gazed up at him in adoration.

"Later, big man."

After a quick fist bump, Omar strolled across the playground, past the basketball court, toward the front where landscapers were cutting and edging the grass surrounding the white brick, one-story building he purchased four years ago. He hadn't been inside since he pulled up earlier, going straight out to the playground because his son wanted to see his friends.

Bradford Enterprises, only five minutes away, was located in a multiple-story building with a sleek glass exterior and was the headquarters for his business ventures, which included real estate development and investing in new and upcoming companies. But this place, the Omar Bradford Foundation, was his baby. The passion project provided all types of assistance but was best known for focusing on kids through mentorship programs, holiday gift-giving, and funding college scholarships.

Inside the building, two eight-year-olds dashed through the lobby, giggling and laughing.

"Hey, hey!" Omar's arm shot out and grabbed the boy in front. "No running in the building. You know better."

"Sorry, Mr. Bradford," they sang.

Typical kids, they continued laughing and jostling each other as they speed-walked down the hall toward the back, probably headed to the playground.

Shaking his head, Omar walked up to the front desk. "Afternoon, Jay. What's good?"

Tall and lanky, with close-cropped hair and a narrow face, Jay had been among the first group of teens when Omar initially set up the mentoring sessions at his foundation. Back then, he'd been a scruffy-looking fifteen-year-old whose mother was at her wits end because he'd been fighting at school, and his grades plummeted as a result.

When Omar hadn't been at practice or playing a game, he spent as much time as he could with him. During those hours, he learned about Jay's insecurities and the anger he experienced after his parents divorced and his father moved to another state.

Now in his mid-twenties and wearing a crisp white shirt and tie, Jay was the face of the Omar Bradford Foundation, the person who greeted people who entered the building looking for help. Because he went from being one of the attendees to working at the foundation, his unique perspective made him empathetic to the parents and young people who walked through the door seeking help.

"I'm all right on this beautiful Monday afternoon. How you doing?" Jay asked.

"All right. You watch the playoffs this weekend?"

"Of course. I think the Hawks can go all the way this year, man."

"You dreaming, bruh. I'm pretty sure my Knicks are going, though." Omar had lived in Atlanta since he started for the Falcons, but after eleven years he still rooted for his hometown team.

"*You* dreaming, bruh," Jay said with a laugh.

"Need I remind you who has two NBA championships?"

"From a long time ago, though, and no worries, we're coming up. Watch, you'll see."

"Uh-huh, keep dreaming."

Omar went toward the back offices and knocked on the door of the executive director.

"Come in," she called.

Inside, his mother sat behind her desk flipping through papers. The open blinds to the left of the desk let in the sun's rays and gave a view of the roadway alongside the property.

"Hey, Ma."

"Hey, pumpkin," his mother replied, looking at him over her glasses.

Dorothy Bradford had been calling him pumpkin since he was a kid and hadn't stopped once, much to his chagrin. But how could he be mad at her? They were practically twins. Everyone said he looked like his mother because of their similar face shape, caramel-toned skin, and green eyes. Though while he was baldheaded, she kept her naturally curly hair trimmed in a short fade.

Without a doubt, the best decision he ever made for the foundation was relocating his parents from New York and giving her the executive director position. For years, she worked in sales for a high-end jewelry store, rising all the way to regional manager before retiring. During that time, she acquired the gift of persuasion through simply talking to people and getting to know them, a skill she used often in her role as executive director of his foundation. She worked well with the board of directors, and in the past two years her ability to talk donors out of millions was indispensable.

"Billie left early for a doctor's appointment," Dorothy continued, referring to their office manager. "But she placed correspondence on your desk that you should take a look at. One of the vendors from the kid's carnival a couple of weeks ago wants to get on our approved vendors list. I think they're fine, but I know you like to take a close look at that kind of thing because we'll be attaching the foundation's name to theirs. Let me know what you want to do. The *AJC* also did a really nice write up about us. They talked about the number of people our scholarship program has helped attend two and four-year colleges. I left a copy on your desk. You should frame it."

The *Atlanta Journal Constitution*, or the *AJC* as Atlantans called it, was the only major daily newspaper in metro Atlanta. "I'll take a look when I go into my office."

Dorothy stood and picked up her clutch. She wore a tailored green dress and a green and purple scarf fashionably tied around her neck. "I'm on my way to a meeting with a donor prospect. Are you coming by for dinner anytime this week? I thought moving here meant I'd see more of my son, but it seems I see you less than when I lived in New York."

"Real subtle, Ma."

His mother had no qualms about making him feel guilty for not spending more time with her and his father. He saw her every Monday when he stopped by the foundation and regularly dropped off Prince to spend time with them, but he was pretty sure even if he went over to their house every night, she would still complain about not seeing him enough.

She shrugged. "I'm just saying, we hardly see you."

"How about I come by for Sunday dinner?"

"Perfect," she said, eyes lighting up with excitement. "I'll make your favorite. Short ribs and mac and cheese."

He could already taste the tender meat and the smoky macaroni and cheese dish. "Could you make a tomato pie too? I haven't eaten one in a long time."

"I certainly can." Dorothy looked very pleased with his request. She spoiled the men in the family with her delicious meals. "I'll see you later," she said, breezing by him out the door.

Omar made his way down the quiet hall to his own office located in the very back corner. Because he didn't spend much time here, the room was small and sparsely furnished with a single desk, a file cabinet, and a couple of chairs. He crossed the carpeted floor and sank into his one splurge, a very nice, copper-colored leather chair from a master craftsman in North Carolina, worth every bit of the three thousand dollars he spent on it.

The foundation had received a number of awards throughout the years, and several of them hung on the wall, but the rest of the certificates and trophies were on full display in the entrance for visitors to see.

From in here, he observed volunteers watching his son and the other kids on the playground. The foundation provided after-school care for parents who couldn't afford it, and in the summer, they offered daycare services and meals. There was plenty to keep the kids preoccupied during the day, including tutoring sessions, a game room, and outdoor activities. Beyond the playground was the baseball diamond, and a basketball court was visible from Billie's office on the other side of the building.

Omar reviewed the correspondence right away and then read the glowing article, pleased the non-profit he started his first year in the league received such high praise.

When his phone beeped, he glanced at the screen.

*Tracy*: Hi

He grinned. He met Tracy a couple of months ago at Avery's Juke Joint with friends. She was a model who hadn't hit the big time yet, but last he heard from her she was in Miami on a shoot, exactly three weeks ago.

*Omar*: wyd?

*Tracy*: Nothing.

*Omar*: Got plans this weekend?

*Tracy*: Maybe.

He liked that she wasn't easy. Being a bit of a challenge and teasing him made their interactions more exciting.

*Omar*: Got an invite to a new restaurant opening on Fri. But if ur busy...

*Tracy*: My schedule suddenly opened up.

He chuckled softly to himself.

*Omar*: I'll come get you at seven.

Tracy: I'll wear those heels you like.

Omar bit his lip, imagining her long, cinnamon-toned legs in the strappy sandals. He was a leg man, and every time he observed a woman in three-inch heels or higher, he couldn't help but admire the sexy arch in the line of their calves.

*Omar*: Do and you might get laid.

*Tracy*: I hope so. [wink emoji]

A knock sounded on the door.

"Come in," he called, glancing up.

The door opened, and the woman who entered made him immediately lose interest in the text conversation.

"Well, look who's here," Omar said, setting down the phone.

She grinned at him.

Dana Lindstrom. His friend. His buddy.

The one woman he couldn't have.

## 2

Damn, she looked good today. But when didn't she? Whether she wore makeup or went barefaced, she was a vision.

Dana was an earthy, plus-size goddess in a sky-blue, ankle-length maxi and toe sandals. Colorful bracelets encircled her wrists, and large colorful earrings—which she at one time told him were 'statement' earrings—hung from her ears.

Today she wore her waist length dreadlocks piled on top of her head in his favorite style, which emphasized the beauty of her face and showed off the tattoo on the back of her neck. From the top to the base, the ladder of motivational words was a succinct embodiment of exactly who Dana was.

*Still I rise.*
*I rise.*
*I rise.*
*I rise.*

"How was Chicago?" he asked, getting up from behind the desk.

He pulled Dana into a warm hug, her soft body settling against his in a comfortable way, and took a deep breath. She

7

always smelled so good—vibrant and refreshing, as if she showered in citrus juices.

"Chicago was Chicago," she replied dismissively, tipping back her head to look up at him with bright brown eyes.

Omar changed the subject because her parents were a sore topic. "What did you bring me?"

"Is that the only reason you're happy to see me?" she asked.

"Now you know better than that."

If she knew the truth, she'd probably slap him. He shouldn't be thinking about his friend naked. So he told himself but couldn't control his thoughts. For years, he squashed his feelings for Dana because deep down he knew he wasn't her type. Frankly, she was too good for him—smart as hell and generous to a fault.

Dana lifted a tin of Garrett's popcorn from the tote she brought in. "Pecan caramel crisp. Don't eat it all at once."

"Challenge accepted," he said, taking the container.

"That wasn't a challenge, you nut. I *don't* want you to eat it all at once."

"Try to stop me." Omar popped the lid and stuffed a handful of popcorn in his mouth. "Damn, this is good," he said with his mouth full.

He could easily order the snack online, but Dana was thoughtful and always took care of others. Without fail, each time she returned from Chicago she brought him back a tin.

Shaking her head in mock disgust, she sat in the chair in front of his desk and crossed her legs. "What did I miss while I was gone for a week?"

"Nothing. Except this. My mother gave it to me today." He handed her the article and then sat in his chair to watch her reaction. While she read, he continued snacking.

"This is wonderful, Omar. You're getting the recognition you deserve."

He could always count on Dana to praise him and give an

encouraging word. She handed back the article, and he returned it to the folder.

"Thanks. You have plans this weekend? I'm going over to my parents' house for Sunday dinner."

"I know Mrs. Bradford is happy she'll have her *pumpkin* with her on Sunday."

"Cut that shit out. Are you free or not?" Omar said irritably.

Dana giggled, her eyes lighting up, and her full lips slanting upward. She was beautiful, but in an understated way. She didn't bring attention to herself by wearing flashy clothes but exhibited her own compelling style.

They met six years ago when he chaperoned a group of seniors, on a Georgia Piedmont Technical College campus tour arranged by his foundation. He chaperoned that day because his scheduled volunteer had canceled.

He met Dana halfway through the tour, a funny and direct English instructor with rich brown skin and dreadlocks. She was one of the few who chatted with the kids in detail about the opportunities afforded by a technical college in lieu of a four-year institution. She discussed English composition and American literature and explained the benefits of the humanities, though most of the kids planned to go into specialized fields.

With two rings in her nose—one in her septum and the other in her left nostril—she'd been so different from the rest of the staff that he was immediately drawn to her spirit and sense of humor. He'd be a liar if he didn't admit to also being attracted to the fullness of her curves. He dated all kinds of women but always appreciated a woman with meat on her bones, and she caught his eye right away. At the time, however, he'd been in a serious relationship.

"Unfortunately, I'm not free on Sunday. Tamika, Layla, and I are going up to Lion Mountain Vineyards in Dahlonega. Layla thinks it's a great place for Tamika's wedding, so we're going to check it out."

"Damn, I need someone to be a buffer between my mother

9

and father always asking questions about my love life. Shit gets old," Omar grumbled.

"Wish I could help you, hon, plus I haven't seen your parents' house yet, but hopefully I'll have a chance to in the near future."

"You're just so busy all the time," he teased.

"Whatever. You're the one with the busy social life, always going to events all over town."

"Speaking of which, wish I'd known you were coming back into town this week."

"I hadn't planned to, but my parents were getting on my nerves with their complaining about this person and that person, problems at work and issues with the neighbors. All they ever do is complain. They're so miserable." She rolled her eyes. "Tommy and Theresa are staying away this summer because they don't want to deal with them."

Dana had four siblings—two older brothers and Tommy and Theresa, fraternal twins eleven years younger than her. She'd partially raised them, and they were both sophomores in college now.

"Why'd you mention that anyway?" she asked.

"I'm going to a restaurant opening on Friday night and would have asked you to come with me if I'd known you'd be back."

Tracy was cool and he'd get laid, but Dana would be more fun.

"I take it you've made other arrangements?" Dana asked.

"Yeah, I did."

She glanced down at her dress and brushed away lint. "Well, I just stopped by to say hi. I have a million things to do before I head home. My refrigerator's empty, so I have to make a trip to the supermarket, but before that, I'm going to the bookstore."

"More books on writing?" Omar asked.

"Yes," she answered with a grimace. "Since I'm not teaching this summer, I'm going to start working on my first full-length novel." She let out a deep breath as if speaking the words out loud took courage, and they probably did.

Dana aspired to become a fiction author. As confident as she was in other areas of her life, writing was the one area where she was insecure. A couple of years ago she submitted her short stories to various contests, with none of them winning any prizes. Since then, she devoted more time to learning the craft of writing, devouring books and YouTube videos about character development and plot structure and everything in between.

"A novel? Look at you." Omar slow-clapped.

"Don't clap yet. I have a lot of work to do, and I'm not sure I'm up to the task."

She stood, getting ready to leave, so Omar stood too.

"I'm sure you are." He didn't doubt for one second Dana would kill it as an author, and as far as he was concerned, she spent too much time preparing to write instead of actually writing.

"If only there was a way to bottle your optimism so I could drink it down whenever I doubt myself." She grinned across the desk at him, and the earth shifted beneath his feet.

Her smile placed a stranglehold on his heart, tightening the muscles in his chest and forcing him to make a conscious decision to breathe. That's what Dana did to him, ever since his drunken ass showed up at her house—all up in his feelings over another woman—and kissed her. To this day he wasn't sure if he was glad he did, or if he wished he'd never known the pleasure of her soft, sweet lips. But he kept his distance, being a good guy and treating her with the respect she deserved while secretly wanting to sully her with every carnal fantasy that crossed his dirty mind.

"I'll see you later," Dana said.

"I'll walk you out."

## 3

Dana watched Omar walk—no strut—down the narrow hall ahead of her in gray slacks and a pale green long-sleeved shirt.

As her eyes followed his movements, she silently lavished praise on his athletic body. He shocked the sporting world when he retired a few years ago and wasn't as physically large as he used to be then, but nonetheless, he had an amazing body with wide shoulders and a thick neck. He turned heads often because people either recognized him as a former Atlanta Falcon or they simply admired his physical beauty.

As a linebacker he'd been known as Omar "Motherfucking" Bradford, a beast on the field whose furrowed brow and piercing eyes planted fear into the hearts of many quarterbacks. Fast on his feet, he achieved among the highest number of sacks in the league during his career. With thick arms and thighs she knew for a fact looked like sturdy tree trunks sprinkled with dark hair, he was exactly the kind of man any woman would notice.

Women noticed him, and he noticed them and went for the same type over and over again—wannabe models and actresses who didn't care anything about the person inside. He could do so much better. All those women cared about was the exterior—a six-two man with a low-cut beard dusting his chiseled jaw and blemish-free caramel-toned skin—but there was so much more to Omar. He had a big heart, especially where kids were concerned, but most of the women he came into contact with only saw the tight body, handsome face, and dollar signs.

"I'm stepping out for a minute, Jay," he said to the young man at the front desk.

Jay acknowledged them with a nod and returned his attention to the computer screen.

Omar held the door open for Dana and she slid past, but not without getting a full blast of his sandalwood cologne, the deep woodsy scent making her imagine being slammed on a mattress and taken aggressively.

*Whew.*

She hid the tremor licking through her body as she led the way to her champagne-colored Camry parked in the lot.

"Is your brother still in town?" she asked, standing beside the car.

Omar squinted against the sun, his green eyes looking greener because of his shirt. "Yeah. He's been vague about when he plans to leave."

Dana had never met Omar's older brother, Cole, who was visiting for the first time from New York. He'd arrived a couple of weeks ago. Omar suspected something was amiss and couldn't figure out what caused him to take an extended trip to Atlanta, but the suspicions about his brother were pure speculation.

When Cole arrived, he brought Omar's son, Prince, from New York with him, and after Father's Day, Omar would take him back.

"How do you feel about him being here?"

His relationship with his brother was similar to her relationship with her parents—tolerable at best.

Omar shrugged. "Doesn't make any difference to me. I see him when I go over to my parents' house. Otherwise, we don't spend time together."

"Eventually, the two of you are going to have to reconcile your relationship."

"It's not me, it's him. He doesn't want to have a real relationship with me, and it took a long time for me to understand and accept the truth. Anyway, you're one to talk. You hardly speak to your parents."

"We speak, but our conversations never go well. Their negativity is draining, and as you know, they're not the most supportive people in the world."

She couldn't remember her parents ever once attending an awards ceremony when she was a kid. They were always too busy at work, so they said, but their lack of support extended into adulthood. By then, she'd become accustomed to being the only person who didn't have family in the audience cheering and clapping for her.

Thank goodness for her friends. When Georgia Piedmont Technical College gave her an outstanding teacher award and a leadership award back in April, her besties and Omar were in the audience, screaming as if she'd won an Oscar, and then they took her out for drinks afterward.

"Aren't we a lovely pair with our family issues," Omar said dryly.

"Can't pick your family..." Dana began.

"But you can pick your friends," Omar finished.

They smiled at each other, and the heat of longing wound a sinuous path beneath Dana's skin and made her nipples tighten. When he looked at her with his eyes soft and head tilted to the side, she wanted to grab him around the neck and kiss him senseless. One would think, after six years his gorgeous face would no longer affect her, but such was not the case.

Omar Bradford did crazy things to her lady parts, and she hoped one day she could meet someone who'd help her get over her pathetic crush on her friend.

"Don't forget, we're defending our championship at Deon's a week from Friday," he said, backing away.

Deon was a cornerback with the Atlanta Falcons, and every few months he and his wife organized a lavish game night at their estate in Buckhead. Last time she and Omar took home the spades tournament trophy.

"I won't. I'm ready to defend our title."

Omar grinned. "Holler if you want to do something before then."

"You call me. You're the one who's in tune with the social scene." Because of his celebrity status, he regularly received tickets to shows and invitations to events all over town.

"Bet. I'll do that," he said.

Dana climbed into her car and watched him walk into the building.

Her friends insisted there was something going on between her and Omar, and she constantly denied the accusation. Partially for her own sanity and partially because she couldn't admit the truth. Three years ago, they shared a kiss she never forgot.

His ex-fiancée, Athena, hurt him deeply when she cheated on him, and he'd discovered her betrayal when he flew to New York to surprise her. When he returned to Atlanta, he showed up drunk to Dana's apartment. She listened to his angry, hurt-filled rants until he fell quiet, burying his face in his hands. She had offered comfort with a friendly embrace, but Omar slipped his arms around her waist and kissed her. She stiffened with shock, and the moments afterward were forever burned into her brain. He'd sobered up real quick and hopped up from the sofa.

*"I'm sorry. I shouldn't have done that," he muttered.*

*"It's okay,"* Dana said, mouth tingling, heart racing.

*"No, it's not. We're friends. I wasn't thinking."*

She pushed down the hurt clawing its way up her throat. *"It's okay. I know you didn't mean it."*

He apologized for kissing her, as if it were the worst thing possible. The sting of those words left an emotional blister that had never gone away.

They didn't talk for weeks after, both keeping their distance from each other. Then one day he showed up at her house and invited her to a club opening. She said yes, and they were back in sync again as if nothing happened. But something did happen, causing a thin crack in the wall of their friendship and forcing her to think of the possibilities with the one man who knew her better than any other.

Seconds. Mere seconds of lip-to-lip contact altered the way she viewed him for good. But nothing was going to happen between them because she put a tremendous amount of effort into hiding her feelings to hold on to their friendship.

Besides, a new Omar had emerged from the wreckage of his relationship with Athena. Dana watched his transformation from monogamous husband-to-be into a man the media referred to as Mr. Casanova. News about his latest bed partners no longer made headlines at the gossip blogs, but he kept a protective wall of thorns around his heart by going through women as if a doctor told him he only had six months to live. She sympathized with the poor women who thought they could win his love. They had a better chance of winning the lottery without buying a ticket.

Dana briefly touched her mouth and relived the moment his lips touched hers several years ago. An onslaught of tingles invaded her body at the memory, and she sighed heavily and then started the car.

"*Friends*, Dana," she muttered.

Surely these feelings would eventually pass.

## 4

Bookstores were one of Dana's favorite places.
She breezed through the doors, feeling as if she were home, and nodded at the clerk at the desk before strolling past the in-store coffee shop to the nonfiction section. There, she zeroed in on the shelves filled with reference material for aspiring and seasoned writers.

With so many bookstores closing in recent years, she was relieved a few independent ones remained open to accommodate people like her. Some of her fondest childhood memories included spending time at the bookstore or the library, browsing the stacks and discovering new authors. Books allowed her to escape the drudgery of her life—growing up poor and taking on the responsibility of being the caretaker of her two younger siblings. Her troubles faded when she spent a few leisurely hours among books. In their pages she was whisked away to foreign lands, traveled through time, or became friends with characters who successfully overcame their problems.

She settled on two books. One gave advice on plotting and the other promised the keys to overcoming writer's block. Once her primary task was completed, she scanned the fiction shelves to reward herself for when she completed the first few chapters of her manuscript.

She eventually found a thick fantasy novel, the first in a series getting rave reviews. Flipping through the pages, she walked slowly toward the front of the store, not paying much attention to her surroundings. She was so enthralled she didn't see the person coming to her left, and bumped into a hard body at the end of one of the rows. Startled, she gasped as she bounced back, the books tumbling from her hands. Almost at the same time, a pair of strong hands gripped her upper arms to keep her from crashing backwards into the bookshelves.

"Excuse me," the man muttered at the same time she said, "I'm sorry."

There was a brief pause, and then they both laughed.

"It was really my fault because I wasn't paying attention," Dana said.

"Neither was I, so we're both guilty." He picked up her books, eyes trained on the top one, and handed them back. "You're a writer?"

"Wannabe writer," she corrected.

"There is no greater agony than bearing an untold story inside you."

Dana blinked, pleased he was familiar with the quote. "Maya Angelou," she said.

"One of the greats, though not without her critics. I once read a scathing critique of her poetry, referring to her writing as —and I quote—'dreadful' and 'shit.' Though they did speak highly of her activism."

"As they should."

They both laughed again. Dana studied him, and he clearly studied her in return. He was tall, a couple of inches over six feet, with caramel toned skin and brown eyes.

"So, you're a fan of Maya Angelou?" she asked.

She herself was a fan, particularly of her poem "Still I Rise," having the words from the poem tattooed on the back of her neck after graduating from college. Her college years had been rough, doing her part to take care of her younger siblings, working almost full time to pay expenses not covered by her scholarship, and navigating the college experience on her own as the first person in her family to attend a university. Then she'd worried about entering the work force with dreadlocks and rings in her nose, but she found a position where she didn't receive judgment and flourished because of her love of the work.

"Honestly, I'm learning more about her. I'm reading classics by people like Langston Hughes, James Weldon Johnson, and Nella Larsen and more history texts, trying to broaden my horizons and learn now what I should have learned years ago."

"That's commendable," Dana said, very impressed. "It's never too late to learn."

"True. So, you're a wannabe writer. What's your real job?"

"I teach English at a local college."

"Helping develop young minds." His pleasant smile and friendly features appealed to her.

"I like to think so. And what do you do?"

He looked thoughtful for a moment and then shrugged. "I'm in between jobs right now. Recently moved here from New York, and I'm taking time to relax and spend time with family I have here. I needed a break from the rat race and the 9-to-5—or rather the 7-to-6 most days."

There were a lot of New York transplants to the Atlanta area, and Dana had picked up on his accent right away.

"Work-life balance can be hard to achieve," she remarked.

"Yes, but we need to prioritize our breaks and take time off. Stress is a silent killer, and if it doesn't kill you, it causes a host of problems." He shook his head as if running through the list. "Anyway, I won't go off on one of my tangents. I noticed one of your books was fantasy. Do you recommend it?"

"I haven't read this author before, but the series is very popular, so I thought I'd give the first book a try. The store has a great fantasy section, as well as a great selection of books in the

African-American Literature section. You should find something you like," she said.

"Actually, I think I already have."

"Oh?" Then his intense expression clued her into the meaning behind the words. "*Oh*," she repeated, cradling her books to her chest as warmth seeped into her limbs.

"I'm Sheldon Reevus." He extended his hand. "Could I interest you in a cup of coffee?"

Dana gave a light laugh and shook his hand.

"I know, you didn't come to the bookstore to get picked up, but that's your fault." Sheldon continued to hold her hand.

"My fault?" She didn't pull away.

"Sure. You're a beautiful woman, *and* I'm going to guess a very smart one too. A lethal combination."

"Intelligent women often turn men off." Dana smoothly removed her hand from his grasp.

"Not this man." Sheldon moved closer and lowered his voice. "Tell you what, give me thirty minutes of your time, and if after thirty minutes you no longer want to be bothered with me, I'll leave you alone and you can walk away."

Dana watched him with narrowed eyes. "Thirty minutes is all you need?"

"Yes, over coffee or whatever you want to drink, and I heard the scones are really good here."

He was slightly charming, not too pushy but making the effort. And he was in a bookstore, for goodness' sake. Definitely a plus.

When her last relationship ended, she decided to take a break from men because she seemed to constantly end up with duds. They were either intellectual types, too aloof or snooty to relax and have a good time, or they were men whose only interests revolved around partying and sex. She longed for a happy median, someone like Omar—a veritable unicorn—who knew how to have a good time but also had interests in business and philanthropy. Maybe she'd found herself another unicorn.

"The chocolate chip cookies are excellent too." Dana pulled out her phone and opened the clock app. "You have a deal. I'm setting the timer for thirty minutes."

He raised his eyebrows. "You don't play around."

"No, I don't." The seconds started counting down.

"Can I at least know the name of the woman I'm going to woo?"

Interesting choice of words. She hadn't been wooed in a long time. So many men didn't make the effort anymore. It was nice to see someone making the effort, and who knows, he might be the distraction she needed to help her get over her feelings for Omar. She would know more in the next twenty-nine minutes.

"My name is Dana. Dana Lindstrom."

## 5

Omar lifted his hand in greeting to the guard as he rolled through the gate at the front of the subdivision where his parents lived in Suwanee. In sweetening the deal to entice them to move from New York, he'd offered to buy them a house.

He himself lived in a condo in Midtown, adequate for his needs as a thirty-three-year-old bachelor. For his parents, however, he purchased a four-sided brick, three-story manor with a master on the main floor, four additional bedrooms on the upper floors, and five and a half baths.

His parents loved the place for different reasons. His mother liked the layout of the house and the privacy afforded by the small community of only thirty houses. His father, Omar Senior, liked having access to the Jack Nicklaus-designed golf course. His passion for the game rubbed off on Omar, and since leaving football, he often played golf with his father.

He parked in the driveway and lifted Prince from the back seat. Jangling his keys as he entered the house, he let Prince run ahead into the kitchen. Right away, the delicious aroma of the meal hit his nostrils, and he practically salivated.

Dorothy wore an apron over her dress and stood at the island, putting the finishing touches on a dish.

"Grandma!" Prince screamed, barreling toward her as if he hadn't seen her in years.

"Hey, baby!" She bent to give him a hug and kiss.

Omar kissed her cheek. "Smells good in here."

"I hope you brought your appetite."

"I see. You prepared a feast."

He reached for a homemade roll, but she smacked his hand, and Omar grunted his displeasure.

"Not before dinner," Dorothy said. "You two go wash up. Your father's in the den watching TV."

Omar sighed heavily and led his son to the bathroom first. Then he went in search of his father and found him in the den making a whiskey sour at the fully stocked bar.

The two-story den was bright and airy, with two sitting areas grouped around mahogany tables. One grouping contained a sectional, armchair, and recliner, while the other consisted of two solid-print armchairs in front of the fireplace.

There was a huge painting of Omar over the stone fireplace in his red Falcons jersey, arms raised overhead as he hollered after sacking the quarterback on the opposing team.

This room led onto the balcony, which contained an exterior fireplace and overlooked a full acre. His parents took full advantage of the outdoor space last winter after they finished renovations. They did a lot of entertaining, inviting over friends to huddle around the warm fire and roast marshmallows or dine on comforting soup with hot cider.

"Hey, Pop."

"Hi, Grandpa!"

"Hey, there." Omar Senior flashed an affectionate smile at his grandson and returned to mixing his drink. "You see how much food your mother's cooking? I thought we were having twenty people over for dinner." He shook his head.

Omar Bradford Senior used to play football when younger and maintained a trim physique. A little shorter than Omar and with a darker complexion, Senior, as everyone called him, had never been good enough to go pro, but his understanding of the game made him an excellent coach from the time Omar started Pee Wee football.

Omar dropped onto the sofa. "You know she enjoys cooking, and you don't mind eating."

"Got that right, but you're taking food with you, or I'll have to eat short ribs, macaroni and cheese, and tomato pie for the rest of the week."

Omar chuckled.

"Drink?" his father asked.

"I'm fine for now. I'll wait until dinner's ready."

"I'll take a drink," Prince piped up.

"You're not ready for this yet. This is a grown up drink," Senior said.

Prince poked out his bottom lip. "Can I go watch TV in grandma and grandpa's room?" he asked Omar.

"Yes. I'll call you when dinner's ready."

Prince took off running.

"Your mini-me's got speed on him. Might be an athlete like you."

"He better. I keep telling him to stop running everywhere, but he don't listen."

"He's like you were at that age. Might as well tell him to stop breathing." His father settled into the recliner. "What's the latest on Kitchen Love? You going to open on time?"

Kitchen Love was the name of a new concept Omar was working on. The farm-to-table restaurant was the first time in a long time he was so excited about a project. In addition to having a typical menu, it would address food insecurity in the community by providing meals free of charge to anyone who walked in off the street and couldn't afford to pay for a meal on their own. The staff would include a mix of paid and volunteer positions, including bussers, waitstaff, and back-of-the-house positions.

"We're almost ready to launch. Only a few more details need to be worked out with the investors, and I have a meeting this week to iron out those plans," Omar replied.

"I'm really proud of you. You're not only interested in making money, you want to make a difference in the world too."

"I learned that from you and Ma."

His father brushed away the comment. "Your mother mostly. You know she can't turn down the opportunity to help a single person," he said with a chuckle and shake of his head.

As Omar was about to agree with his father, his brother Cole walked into the room, and his presence seemed to dim the sun and turn the air gray.

"Omar," Cole said by way of greeting.

"Cole."

At thirty-eight, Cole's caramel complexion matched Omar's, but his eyes were brown, and he had a head full of low-cut hair. Both men were a couple inches over six feet, but Cole had a slighter build.

His brother sank onto the sectional. "Think I'm gonna stick around for another month or so. I might move here."

Senior swung his head in Cole's direction, an indication the announcement was new information.

"Really?" Omar said. "What brought that on?"

Shrugging, Cole said, "I like Atlanta. There's plenty to do, and the weather is nice. Giving it some thought, that's all."

"What about your job in New York?" Senior asked.

Cole worked at a property management firm. As a manager, his portfolio included a mix of properties with a wide range of rents.

"I'll figure out the details later."

Something was up, but Cole was sneaky and wouldn't divulge the information before it was time, and certainly not to Omar.

There had always been a weird rivalry between them, which kept them from being close. As a kid, Omar idolized his older brother and, for a long time, did almost anything for a better relationship with him—including investing in a couple of his failed businesses over the years. Cole made it clear he never really wanted a relationship, though, and Omar realized the issues went deeper. Cole was jealous, though he never explicitly said as much, and nothing Omar did could change Cole's resentment, so he finally gave up.

Omar's relationship with his fellow football players was much better. He formed a bond with them and experienced the true meaning of brotherhood, where they looked out for each other and trained together, and when he was a rookie, he lived with a couple of the guys for two years.

Academically, Cole had always done better than Omar. Omar used to struggle with his school work, and if not for his athletic ability, he was pretty certain he would have been held back at least once during his middle school or high school years.

His businesses might have failed, but Cole never had a hard time getting work. He was charming and knowledgeable about a range of topics, enough to BS his way into several good-paying jobs. However, while he excelled in his professional life, his personal life was always chaotic and filled with one disaster after another. He married young and then divorced within a year. After initially setting up his own phone repair business, he went bankrupt because of mismanagement. He eventually earned his broker license and got a job at a property management firm. Four years ago the office manager sued the company and Cole, alleging sexual harassment. They settled out of court for an undisclosed sum, but he kept his job.

Now here he was hanging out in Atlanta as if he didn't have a job in New York, and even more shocking was his talk about moving here. Was he running from something?

"If you're serious about moving here, let me know," Omar said. "I know a lot of people and could get you in touch with the right folks to get established here."

Several beats passed as Cole studied him from the other end of the sectional. "I might take you up on your offer."

Senior cleared his throat. "You're welcome to join us when we play golf. Might be fun, the three of us out there together."

Cole shook his head. "I can count on one hand how many times I've played golf. It's a rich man's game."

"Nonsense. We'll teach you everything you need to know, won't we, Omar?"

Omar immediately nodded. "Absolutely."

Laughing, Cole said, "Okay, you've twisted my arm. Next time you play, include me. Playing golf will give me something else to do besides sightseeing."

"Excellent." Senior's gaze connected with Omar's, and a message passed between them—one of hope of potential changes to come.

"Dinner is ready," Dorothy said from the doorway.

"Good, I'm starving." Senior hopped up from the recliner with the agility of a much younger man and was the first one out the door.

Omar called his son and soon the family was gathered around the table. His father led the prayer and then they dived into the delicious food, passing plates around, laughing and talking like a normal family should.

Cole's response to Omar's and Senior's offers lifted Omar's spirits. He remembered Dana's comment last week and thought maybe, just maybe, Cole's visit presented the opportunity for them to finally mend their relationship.

## 6

"I'm so happy to see you and your brother get along so well," Dorothy whispered, standing at the back door leading to the driveway. "Cole's visit was a good decision, don't you think?"

Though she didn't verbalize her thoughts much, Omar knew the strained relationship between him and his brother caused his mother deep concern.

Cradling a sleeping Prince against his shoulder, Omar replied, "I'm starting to think so. Any idea how long he plans to stay?"

His mother shook her head. "He's been very vague, but he's welcomed as long as he wants to. You're both in your thirties, and it's time to set aside your differences. Make the best of his visit here."

"I'll try, Ma."

He would do anything for his mother. Her encouragement and unconditional love over the years helped him excel in football and become the man he was today. Whether she wanted him to walk across hot coals or perform the much more difficult task of mending the relationship with his brother, he would make a sincere effort to try.

"Good night," Dorothy said quietly, waving as Omar walked the short distance to the Escalade.

Earlier, he placed the food they were taking home in the back. With all the leftovers his mother packed for them, he and Prince would have dinner for a couple of days.

He climbed in the vehicle and started out of the subdivision. When he hit the highway, he turned on soft music for the drive, gaze flicking to Prince slouched in his car seat, mouth partially open. He looked like a little angel and Omar's chest tightened with love. Sometimes he couldn't believe he had a kid, and such a good kid. He definitely hit the jackpot with his little mini-me.

His phone rang and his ex-fiancée's name showed on the screen. Athena, Prince's mother. Omar hit the Bluetooth button and answered.

"Hi, checking in to see how the two of you are doing," Athena said.

"I'm in the car. Prince is in the back seat, asleep. We went to my parents' house for dinner and left about ten minutes ago."

"Lucky Prince, getting all that good home cooking. I miss your mom's Sunday dinners."

Omar didn't respond, keeping his eyes trained on the road ahead and switching lanes. Every now and again, Athena dropped comments into their conversations to remind him of how they used to be, but he had no desire to reminisce with her about the past. If she hadn't cheated on him, nothing would have changed, and he only found out about her other man by chance.

Prince was almost a year old when Omar let the team know he was retiring at the end of the season. They tried to talk him out of his decision by offering more money and bonuses, and his agent said he'd work harder at getting more endorsement deals, but none of those offers appealed to him because his mind was already made up.

He had talked to his parents and Dana in detail about the decision, and it was the right choice for him. Jason Brown quit football around the same age to become a farmer, so why couldn't Omar do the same? He had plenty of money, and football had been good to him—paying his way through school and giving him a high salary that allowed him to start several businesses and his nonprofit. He was, however, ready to move on. Walking away would allow him more time for his business ventures and the Omar Bradford Foundation, which meant he could expand his empire and the influence of his charitable works.

While he lived in Atlanta, Athena and Prince lived in New York, but they agreed she would move to Atlanta after the season was over, and then they'd get married.

He couldn't make the date of Prince's first birthday because of a prior engagement, so he showed up two days early as a surprise, calling Athena from the airport to let her know he was on his way. They spent the day celebrating Prince's birthday, but a bigger surprise awaited him when he was about to go to sleep. He found another man's boxers tangled in the sheets on their bed—the bed he shared with her.

First she tried to convince him the underwear belonged to him, which made no sense since he hadn't been home in months. Then she tried to convince him it belonged to her brother, whom she gave the master bedroom when he visited. He never believed her, and their engagement ended with plenty of tears and her begging him not to go.

At the time, one of his friends accused him of looking for a way out of the relationship. Maybe. By then he and Dana were very close, and he struggled to reconcile his feelings for her with his feelings for Athena, whom he'd known longer, planned to marry, and was the mother of his child.

Athena continued. "I called because your finance manager left a message saying you're increasing the amount you give me for Prince each month. That's not necessary. You give me plenty already."

Omar frowned as he switched lanes. Most of his friends and acquaintances complained about the amount of money they paid to their baby mamas and grumbled whenever asked for money above and beyond the monthly child support. Athena may have her faults, but she never asked for extra money and did an amazing job making sure Prince was taken care of out of the funds he deposited into her account each month. He was lucky and didn't have any complaints about how she took care of their son.

"Costs go up, and I've been giving you the same amount since he was born. He's four now, and the increase is well overdue."

"If you're sure..."

"I'm sure," he said firmly.

"All right," she said unenthusiastically. "While I have you on the phone, I wanted to let you know I'm thinking about visiting Atlanta a few days before Father's Day, if you don't mind. I haven't been there in a while, and I'd like to go out, do a little shopping, maybe see some sights and spend time at your parents' house. Your mom mentioned Kitchen Love will open the same week as Father's Day, so I might stick around for the opening. Is that okay?"

"Sure, fine by me. Are you definitely coming?"

"I'm not sure yet. My visit won't cause you any problems?"

Omar gritted his teeth. He hated how she always beat around the bush instead of getting to the point. So different from Dana, who said whatever she was thinking.

"Ask me what you want to ask, Athena," he said.

There were a few seconds of silence.

"If..." Her voice wavered. "If there's another woman, I wouldn't want to cause any problems..."

She knew he dated because every now and again his name appeared in a magazine or on a gossip blog with the name of his current companion. Thankfully, those articles didn't appear as often since he was no longer a hot celebrity.

"I don't have a girlfriend, but if I did, I'd make sure she understood there was nothing to worry about," he snapped. The words sounded harsher than he'd intended, but Athena needed to understand she could not create problems for him. As far as he was concerned, she was a non-issue.

"Omar, don't you sometimes wonder—"

"No." He gripped the leather steering wheel, hating the position she was putting him in, forcing him to be blunt to drill home that nothing could ever happen between them again. "Don't do this, Athena. We've been here before, and I've made it clear every single time that we can't go back. I'm not trying to hurt you. You're the mother of my son, but you can't keep bringing up the past. Do you understand?" He kept his voice firm.

"Yes, I understand," she said quietly.

The hurt in her voice tore at him because at one time he had loved her and planned to marry her. She somehow managed to make him feel guilty though he was simply telling her the truth and setting boundaries for their relationship—boundaries she tried to circumvent at random times.

"Anything else?" Omar asked.

"No. I'll let you know if I decide to come to Atlanta."

"Sounds good. Talk to you later." Omar hung up before she could say another word.

## 7

"What are you doing here?" Dana asked.

Omar stood on her doorstep.

Pursing his lips, he slowly shook his head. "You did forget."

Hair piled on her head and glasses perched on her nose, Dana stared at him in confusion and then gasped, covering her mouth. "Game night."

"Yeah, game night."

His gaze assessed her oversized shirt, leggings, and socks. "Please tell me you forgot, because if you're going dressed like that..."

"Hush." Dana swung away from the door and dashed over to the sofa where she'd been engrossed in her story.

After getting stuck on a scene for over an hour, she'd left the desk and moved to the sofa with a notebook and pen. One of the books she purchased at the bookstore suggested writing long hand to get rid of writer's block. The tip worked, and she quickly wrote ten pages as the words poured out of her.

"What were you doing?" Omar asked.

"Writing."

Dana scraped up her notebook and pen and dumped them on

the desk in the corner. Then she turned off the computer and faced him. Of course he looked magnificent, filling the room with his presence in dark slacks and a black, fitted polo shirt lying like a second skin over the contours of his chest.

"Give me fifteen—no, twenty minutes—and I'll be ready to go."

Omar pulled out his phone, and she knew he was setting his timer.

"Is that really necessary?" Dana grumbled as she hurried past him and headed for the stairs.

"You do it to me, I do it to you," he said, amusement in his voice. "You have twenty minutes." He held up the face of his phone so she could see the countdown had begun.

She shot a nasty glare in his direction, and a burst of laughter left his throat before she raced up the stairs.

Luckily, she didn't have to shower, so she should be able to meet the twenty-minute deadline. After screwing up because she forgot about their plans, she'd never hear the end of it if she was late. They mercilessly teased each other at the slightest shortcoming.

Dana ditched her glasses and changed bras, putting on a black one that lifted her bosom. Then she wiggled into a black, open-bust bodysuit and buttoned her figure-clinging denim dress, leaving the top button undone to give a hint of the great cleavage created by the bra.

She kept her hair piled on her head but added large gold earrings. With lipstick, a little mascara, and a pair of white tennis shoes, she was ready to go with minutes to spare.

She grabbed her cross-body bag and ran downstairs. "I'm ready—"

To her surprise, Omar sat on the sofa with her notebook in hand and was reading the words on the page. He looked up, and before he said a word, there was a pregnant pause as his gaze scanned her appearance. She couldn't define what she saw in his expression, but his eyelids lowered, as if to hide his thoughts, and heat burst onto her cheeks and neck.

Dana snatched away the book. "You can't read my story."

Omar brought his gaze—almost reluctantly—from her chest up to her eyes. "Why not?"

"Because it's a rough, rough draft."

He stood up and towered over her. "Give it back. I'm not finished."

"I didn't give you permission to read my work," Dana said, holding the notebook behind her and backing toward the far wall.

"You didn't say I couldn't."

"I am now."

"Too late."

Her back hit the wall, and he didn't stop coming. He stepped right up to her, crowding her against the Sheetrock.

"Give it," he said, holding out one hand.

"Nope." She stared up at him in defiance.

Their eyes locked in a silent battle.

"I'm going to count to three," he warned.

"You can count all you want," Dana said, trying desperately to ignore the pleasing scent of sandalwood invading her nostrils.

"One."

"This is my work. You need my permission to read it." She rolled the book into a cylinder and tightened her fingers around it, fighting the urge to raise up on tiptoe and press her nose into his neck.

"Two."

"What exactly do you plan to do, huh? I'm going to fight you."

"Three," Omar said with finality.

He tugged her toward him and her breasts smashed into his chest. Dana let out a low screech filled with alarm but also the thrill of excitement. Omar reached behind her, and she twisted to avoid his hands, but his reach was long. He grabbed her wrists and forcibly curled her arms in front of her body. Darn, he was strong.

He easily tugged away the notebook. "Thank you," he said.

"Give it back!" Dana jumped, but he held it above her head out of reach.

"I only have a few more pages to go."

He walked calmly back to the sofa, as easy as you please, while she stayed in the same spot for a few seconds, trying to get her shallow breathing under control because being so close to him deeply affected her. He, on the other hand, seemed perfectly fine.

She settled on the other end of the sofa and watched him read with a knot in her stomach. His expressions alternated between a blank face and deep frowns.

When he finished, he set down the book.

"Did she kill her husband?" he asked.

"I'm not saying."

"Damn, what an opening. Excellent." He placed the book in the space between them.

"Really?"

Dana was so self-conscious about her work, she never let anyone read her stories. She guarded them like the gold at Fort Knox, so his compliment meant a lot.

"Hell, yeah. You know I don't read much, but your story kept my attention."

"You're biased because I'm your friend."

"You've known me long enough to know I wouldn't pay you a compliment if I didn't mean it. It's a really strong start."

Dana let out a quiet breath of relief. He was her cheerleader. She wasn't allowed to doubt herself in his presence. He also spoiled her—as much as she let him. She was so used to taking care of others and spending on others, but he didn't hesitate to take care of her in small ways—dinners out, tickets to events.

For years, she toyed with the idea of attending a writing

retreat but didn't know if she was good enough. Maybe she didn't need to be so worried after all.

"I've done research on writing retreats, and I'm thinking about attending one in Colorado. For two weeks, I and other aspiring writers would get to work with one of the best writing coaches in the business."

"You sound like you're not sure you want to go," Omar said.

"I do want to go."

"Then do it."

With airfare, lodging, food, and the training, the trip cost thousands of dollars. She didn't want to admit her concerns about spending so much money. What if an emergency came up?

"I'll think about it," she said.

Omar studied her for a minute, then he said, "You have to do things for yourself too, Dana."

"Yes, I know. You've told me a thousand times."

"Then why don't you? In all the years we've known each other, I've never seen you take a real vacation. Every year, you go back to Chicago and spend time with your parents, and you take a short trip here and there, like the time you went to DC with Layla. But that's it."

"Can we skip the lecture tonight?" Dana stood, ready to go.

He remained seated. "Dana—"

"I know you don't understand, but not everyone has a bunch of cash lying around, and you know I don't have only myself to think about. Tommy or Theresa might need help, and if I splurge on the trip, they'll have to do without."

"Splurge? The retreat isn't a splurge, Dana. You want to be a writer, and it takes work. You should be able to take the necessary steps if you want or need to." Omar looked steadily at her. "You're not their mother," he said quietly.

She and Omar were alike because neither wanted kids. Though he already had a son whom he loved, he didn't want any more children and got a vasectomy soon after. Meanwhile, she made the decision a long time ago to be child-free but still felt responsible for her younger siblings.

"No, I'm not their mother, but I don't want them to go through what I did. I want them to see the world and have amazing life experiences, and if I can help, I want to. They shouldn't be stuck the way I was, having to live vicariously through characters in a book!"

She became emotional when she thought about her upbringing. No, Tommy and Theresa weren't her kids, but there was nothing wrong with helping them financially, and no real difference between what she did for them and Omar taking care of his parents, buying them a house, or investing in his brother's failed businesses.

The only difference was, his bank account was larger than hers.

Omar pushed up off the sofa. "Let me pay for your trip."

She suspected he'd say that. "No."

"Dana, we're friends, and I can afford it."

"I can afford it too. When the time is right."

"Would you let me—"

"I don't want to talk about this anymore! Can we go have fun? Please?"

Omar rubbed a palm over his bald head as if exhausted from the conversation. "Fine. The conversation is over. *For now.*" He looked pointedly at her.

Dana gladly accepted the temporary reprieve, and they left her townhouse. Omar opened the door for her, and she climbed into the Escalade.

It was her favorite of his vehicles. He loaned it to her for a week once when her car was in the shop, and she'd been spoiled by the roomy interior, the high-end sound system, and the navigation screen. There was even a console refrigerator where she had kept chilled water and juice while running errands around town. Man, she missed this car.

She watched him circle the front and climb in, and they took off. Omar drove with one hand on the wheel and eyes trained on the traffic before him. Because of their brief argument, an awkward silence filled the car.

To ease the tension, Dana asked, "How was dinner at your parents'?"

He glanced at her. "I survived," he replied.

He was talking to her. A good sign.

"They didn't give you too much of a hard time about your love life?"

A smile tugged at the corner of his mouth, which meant they were definitely in a better place than ten minutes ago.

"Nah, they were on their best behavior. Interesting enough, so was Cole. There's a tiny chance he and I might be able to have a better relationship. My dad invited him to go golfing with us, and he accepted."

"Wow, progress."

"We'll see. Keep your fingers crossed for me."

"How was the restaurant opening?"

Stroking his bearded chin, Omar replied, "A mixed bag. Good energy, but they weren't ready for the crowd. Food tasted fine, but the service was terrible. I think the owners underestimated how much staff they needed, so the food came out of the kitchen slowly, and they brought me the wrong dish for dinner. I ate it, though, because by then I was starving. I got someone's salmon and somebody got my trout. The whole experience made me think about Kitchen Love and how I need to make sure we have plenty of staff to handle service opening night."

"Better to have too many people than not enough."

They rode in silence for a few minutes.

"You're not still mad at me, are you?" Dana asked.

He let out a little laugh, and the same corner of his mouth curled into a smile, while he glanced at her from the corner of his eye. She wondered if he had any idea how sexy he looked.

"You know I can't stay mad at you."

His voice had dipped low and vibrated in the air, leaving her skin peppered with goosebumps. She smoothed a hand over her thigh to negate the effect and hide the trembling of her fingers.

"I appreciate your offer to pay for my trip, and if my situation changes, I'll let you know."

He nodded slowly. "I'd do anything for you. I hope you know that." He kept his eyes on the road, but she didn't miss the gravity of his words.

"I do."

## 8

Deon and his wife Rebecca lived in a multi-million-dollar home in an affluent Buckhead neighborhood filled with more multi-million-dollar homes. Their brown, Tudor-style house seemed to rise up out of the concrete at the end of a long driveway brightened by landscape lights and lights in every window.

Game night at their house included a spades tournament with a one-hundred-dollar buy-in. Last time Omar covered his and Dana's fee, and when they emerged the victors, he split the sixteen-hundred-dollar cash prize evenly with her. While the money was merely pocket change to him, Dana used her winnings to help Tommy and Theresa cover school expenses.

The basement of Deon's house was crowded, but as soon as they walked in, Dana spotted the host. During the off-season, the showy athlete had dyed his hair blond, in sharp contrast to his mahogany skin.

"Look who's here. The tournament champs!" Deon bellowed as soon as he spotted them.

He came over, and he and Omar greeted each other with a complicated dap, slapping their palms together, snapping, and ending with a fist bump.

"I'm coming for your trophy," Deon said, briefly hugging Dana.

"You can have the trophy when you pry it out of my cold, dead hands," Dana said.

"Oh damn, she already talking shit. It's on, baby, it's on!" Deon hollered.

Dana and Omar laughed at his antics and then made their way over to the cashier. Omar paid the one-hundred-dollar fee and so did Dana. Afterward, they snacked on heavy hors d'oeuvres but limited the amount of liquor they drank so they could keep clear heads.

Guests crowded around the roulette table, played cards, or chatted at the bar. The company catering the event supplied servers who took food and beverage orders from the guests, and anyone not playing a game sat at the tables eating or hovered near the bar chatting and drinking.

When the spades tournament started, four teams participated, half as many as last time. Walking over to their table, Omar whispered, "We're going to kick their asses."

"Most definitely," Dana agreed.

They were both competitive and being the defending champs fueled adrenaline in their veins.

They sat across from each other, and after the dealer distributed the cards, Dana examined hers and looked at Omar.

"How many you want to bid?" he asked.

"I have four and a possible," she said.

He nodded, a grin spreading across his face. "I have four."

"Nine," they said in unison.

Not only were they competitive, they were so in tune, they practically read each other's mind.

The game started, cards dropping quickly in the center of the table because of the ten-second rule. Omar and Dana ended up with the nine books as expected, but the last one was a bit of a fluke. Dana looked at the cards and shook her head, and when her ten of diamonds walked, the players and the spectators hooted and hollered.

"Goddammit!" said her opponent to the right.

She and Omar cackled and high-fived over the table and then prepped for the next game.

Over the course of the night, two teams were eliminated, leaving Dana and Omar and two brothers—Mario and Jayson. Earlier, the brothers won their game with a flourish, with Mario standing up from the table and slamming down the winning card. They were as cocky as Dana and Omar, but she was certain they could beat them.

The final game began with a lot of tension. Dana and Omar eyed each other across the table, carefully bidding each hand as a small crowd of spectators encircled them to watch the final match up. The game was close and essentially came down to the final play, when each team held one card in their hands.

Dana said a silent prayer and played her card, a nine of diamonds. Mario put down a ten of hearts and looked at his brother with hopeful eyes. Omar placed a four of spades on the stack, and Dana inhaled sharply, careful not to smile but crossing her fingers under the table. Could they win again? She sure hoped so. It all depended on the card in Jayson's hand. She glanced at him and caught the fleeting look of disappointment on his face. Her foot bounced excitedly under the table, and she held her breath.

When Jayson tossed the Ace of diamonds on the table, their audience erupted into a mixture of cheers and groans.

Dana jumped to her feet and screamed, "Yes!" Hands in the air, she danced in a circle while doing a body roll. "We won… we won…" she sang.

Deon shook his head in disgust. "Y'all be cheating, man."

Omar put him in a headlock. "I'll take the cash and the trophy before we leave, thank you very much."

He looked at Dana and grinned.

She grinned back and gave him a fist bump.

Omar and Dana strolled to her front door.

"Deon hates us now," he said.

"I know. Did you hear his crazy self when he said he was going to ban us from coming to his game night?"

"I heard him," Omar laughed.

At the door, Dana held the gold trophy above her head and then slowly lowered it to her lips. Omar chuckled at her theatrics.

Hugging the trophy to her chest, she said, "You played well tonight, partner. I'm three hundred dollars richer than when I left the house earlier." Her eyes were glowing.

"How about we go out to celebrate tomorrow night? My treat." Whenever he spent time with Dana, he never wanted the night to end, and dinner tomorrow night was one way to extend their time together.

"I can't. I have plans. Raincheck?"

"Sure. What are you and your girls getting into tomorrow night?"

"Actually, I don't have plans with them. Remember the guy I told you I met at the bookstore? We're going out tomorrow night."

The night immediately lost some of its shine.

"Oh. This is what, your second date?"

"First. I don't count the bookstore since that's where we met."

"He's from New York, right?"

"Mhmm."

"What kind of work does he do?"

"He's in between jobs right now. I like him because he has diverse interests," she continued, "and we talk about everything. We read the same types of books too, but I don't want to say too much."

Something in her voice made him pay closer attention. Over

the years, he'd heard Dana talk about her various boyfriends or men she slept with, but the conversations were always in passing, and she never seemed to get too attached to the men. In fact, she barely tolerated them most of the time. She spoke about this guy in a different way. Not flippantly but with genuine interest, which made his gut tighten.

Omar stuffed his hands in his pants pockets. Dana was smart as hell, and most of her exes were smart—professors, doctors, scientist types. This man sounded like he was more of the same. Someone she met in a bookstore and struck up a conversation with about old novels and history books. Nothing like Omar's dumb ass, a jock who spent most of his academic life doing the bare minimum to get by.

"Why don't you want to talk about him?" he asked.

"I know this sounds silly, but he's the first man in a long time who's made me feel... something. I don't want to jinx it, but I'm kind of... ecstatic."

*Ecstatic*. Huh. She'd never used that word before in reference to a man. A ball of dread settled in his belly.

"I thought you were going to take a break from men for a while," he said.

"I was, but he made me reconsider. Anyway, this is completely brand new. We might go out tomorrow and have a horrible time and hate each other and decide to never see each other again. For now, I'm excited to see what happens." She lifted her right shoulder in a negligent shrug.

He should say something—share encouraging words, wish her the best. Yet he couldn't bring himself to do it, though Dana deserved a good man.

"I'm going to head home. I'll catch up with you later," he said.

"G'night. Drive carefully."

Omar went back to his SUV but sat in the lot, unable to leave. He needed to be near Dana for a little bit longer, and he needed to think. How many more times would he have to stand on the sidelines and watch her get involved with other men? It was getting to the point where the mere mention of another man made him ragey. And who the hell was this new guy, and what made him so special?

The light downstairs went off and a minute later one upstairs went on, and his imagination went haywire. He imagined her disrobing, taking her time to release each of the buttons on her dress, one by one. Would she change into night clothes or sleep naked, like he did?

Omar swore and started the vehicle.

"Go home," he muttered and pulled out of the lot.

## 9

"I can't believe I went on a nighttime tour of a cemetery," Sheldon said, shaking his head.

Laughing, Dana sat across from him at their table, on the patio bar of Six Feet Under Restaurant Pub and Fish House, giving them a good view of Oakland Cemetery across the street.

"Tell the truth, did you like it? Did you learn a lot?"

He nodded, smiling across at her. "Yes to both."

"Then my job is done."

At the bookstore, Sheldon gave her his number and encouraged her to call. When she finally did and agreed to meet up, he asked for a restaurant recommendation, and she suggested Six Feet Under. They served popular seafood options like fish tacos, fish and chips, and oysters and offered a good beer selection. But the food wasn't the only reason she suggested they come here.

Across the street from the restaurant was Oakland Cemetery, a 42-acre Atlanta landmark built in 1850. Famous Georgians buried there included Maynard Jackson, the first Black mayor of the city, Carrie Steele Logan, a former enslaved woman who established the first African-American orphanage, and Margaret Mitchell, Pulitzer Prize-winning author of *Gone With the Wind*. Since Sheldon was a history buff, she figured he'd enjoy the tour.

"I have a feeling whenever I'm with you, I'm going to learn something," he said.

Minutes later, a mug of beer sat in front of each of them.

"To a great night," Sheldon said, holding up his glass.

Dana touched her glass to his.

"I have to admit, I didn't think you'd call," he said, after taking a sip of beer.

"Why?" she asked, surprised.

"Don't know. I kind of got the feeling you might not be into me."

"Well, let me assure you, I am definitely into you, and that's why I called."

"Good. Because I'd like to see more of you. I feel like we have a lot in common."

"We do," she agreed.

"What are your thoughts about marriage?" he asked, leaning closer. His eyes locked on her as he awaited an answer.

"Whoa, going for the big questions right away," Dana said with a laugh, rearranging her long skirt under the table.

Sheldon shrugged. "I like to lay my cards on the table. I married young, and it didn't work out, but I'm not afraid to get married again. I *want* to get married again."

"I've never been married, but it's definitely something I would like to do—when I meet the right person."

"Okay." His sat back.

"That's not a jab at you," Dana said hurriedly, "but we're in the very early stages of this thing... whatever we're doing."

"Can I be honest with you?"

"Of course."

He tapped a finger on the tabletop. "When I met you in the bookstore, I wasn't completely sure I wanted to stay in Atlanta. I considered going back to New York."

"And now?"

"I'm definitely going to stay," he answered, looking at her

with meaning, clearly indicating she was a major factor in his decision-making.

Dana didn't know what to say. She preferred to be open and direct in most of her interactions, and in the silence, she sipped her beer as she considered how to respond.

"We're alike in a lot of ways," Sheldon said. "Same taste in books, same sense of humor, and I believe if given the opportunity to spend more time in each other's company, we could have a future together. Is that something you see as a possibility?"

The answer should be easy, yet Dana hesitated. She *did* like him. While this was officially their first date, their conversations on the phone and the one at the coffee shop had been easy and fluid. She liked his sense of humor, and he seemed nice enough.

Yet when he mentioned a future and marriage, her mind immediately went to Omar. What was he doing tonight? Did he have a date? Though she enjoyed her time with Sheldon, she also enjoyed her time with Omar too. He expanded her horizons and exposed her to activities she might not normally try.

One year, he talked her into zip lining at Lake Lanier. She almost chickened out when her turn came to zoom across the cable, but Omar stood right there, whispering encouraging words in her ear until she mustered the courage to launch. Zip lining had been one of the scariest, most exhilarating experiences, and she'd returned three more times since then.

"I wouldn't want to take anything off the table," Dana replied to Sheldon, "but you're putting a lot of pressure on our new relationship. We hardly know each other, and I don't want you to base your decision-making on the potential of what we *could* have."

"Fair enough. I accept your answer, but I have one more question for you, if you don't mind. Then I'll lay off the serious talk."

"Okay," Dana said, bracing herself.

"How do you feel about kids?"

Kids. A touchy subject for sure, and she would have to tread carefully because so many people didn't understand her decision to remain child-free.

"I love children..."

"But?" Sheldon prompted with a furrowed brow.

"I've thought long and hard about this and decided I don't want to have children of my own. Ever."

His eyebrows shot higher in surprise. "I didn't expect that answer."

"Most people don't. They look at someone like me, who's only thirty-one years old, and are certain I would want to have kids. Everyone wants them, right? The thing is, I feel like I've already raised some kids, and I don't want any more."

He sat forward and leaned on his forearms. "You know you have to explain, right?"

Dana nodded. "When I was eleven years old, my younger brother and sister—fraternal twins, were born. I have two older brothers, the closest one in age to me is three years older. As the only girl, my parents expected me to take over the responsibility of watching my younger siblings because they worked a lot, and those expectations continued all the way through getting my masters and graduating from college."

"And you got your masters at twenty-one, correct?"

"Correct." Dana took college classes while in high school, so by the time she graduated, she was essentially a sophomore in college.

"Why English?"

"Reading was an escape for me when I was a child, and I fell in love with story-telling, and sentence structure, and words, and how they convey emotions. Once I became responsible for my younger siblings, it became more important. On the weekends, I took them to the library with me. We walked half a mile and caught two buses each way, but I needed my books. I still read everything I can get my hands on," she added with a laugh.

"I came late to reading for leisure. I did the necessary reading for school, but sports were the most important thing in my household, and I was never very good at them. My younger brother... well, he was a star athlete and got all the attention."

Bitterness crept into his voice. Dana wanted to delve deeper, but he continued talking.

"Anyway, I sort of stumbled into reading. I was at a friend's house, and his son left one of the books assigned by his teacher on the table—*Their Eyes Were Watching God* by Zora Neale Hurston. Changed my life. Ever since then, I've been on a bender to get my hands on as many Black lit books from that era I can. But enough about me. Please, continue. What happened after you received your masters?" He lifted the beer mug to his lips.

"As soon as the diploma was in my hand, I packed up my belongings and moved to Atlanta. It was a drastic decision, and one I didn't take lightly. But I needed to leave because for ten years, my life wasn't my own. Even when I was in school and needed to study for exams, my parents expected me to take care of Tommy and Theresa, my younger brother and sister. When I finally left home, my parents were not pleased. To this day I think they resent me for leaving, but I didn't have a choice."

She got away, escaped. Meanwhile, they remained in the same neighborhood and the same apartment complex she lived in as a child, their lives frozen in time.

Dana took a deep breath and released it. "As far as I'm concerned, I was a mom for ten years. I love my younger brother and sister to death, and we're very close to this day, but my relationship with my parents is not so great. I will say, being a surrogate mother taught me a lot but also drained me."

"And that's why you don't want kids of your own."

"Exactly."

"What if you met a man with children?"

"Do you have children?"

"No, but I'm curious to know how you'd handle such a situation."

"If I met a man with kids, I would become a stepmother and

help him raise his children. As for wanting to start a family of my own or having kids with someone I marry, that's not going to happen."

He fell silent, and she wondered if her choice was a deal breaker for him. She would completely understand because anyone who expected her to have children would learn real quick they were a deal breaker for her.

When she thought about being with someone with children, she always thought about Omar and his son Prince. Though she didn't want children of her own, being a stepmother to Prince was not an issue, mostly because he was Omar's son.

But why bother thinking in those terms? She and Omar were never going to be a couple.

"I was never forced to take care of my younger brother, so I don't know what you went through, but from what you've told me, I'm not surprised the experience influenced your decision. Thank you for your honesty," Sheldon said.

"Did my answer change how you feel about me? About us?" She became a bit apprehensive because she did like Sheldon. She didn't know why he was different compared to her most recent relationships. Maybe she needed to believe he was different, and all the others failed because they weren't right for her. Or maybe, if she looked deeply enough, she'd discover she simply longed to be with someone who finally made her stop pining for Omar.

He looked thoughtful for a moment and then shook his head. "No. What you said doesn't change my opinion about you."

"And you're not thinking you can change my mind, are you? I've run across men who believe too much in their persuasive powers."

"I'm not that kind of man. If not having children of your own is your decision, I understand, and it doesn't change my opinion of you."

Dana relaxed in the chair. Sheldon was definitely different, because when this part of the conversation came up, she was either called selfish, told she would change her mind, or told the right man could change her mind. None of those comments came from his mouth, and she appreciated his open-mindedness.

After the meal, they skipped dessert and instead stopped for donuts before going back to Dana's townhouse. She unlocked the door and turned to face him.

"I enjoyed myself tonight," she said softly.

"So did I."

Sheldon bent his head and gave her a kiss, starting with a gentle peck. When she didn't pull back, he wrapped his arms around her and deepened the kiss. Groaning, he shifted his hands to her bottom and tugged her closer until his erection hit her lower abdomen.

Dana pressed her hands against his chest and pulled back.

"What?" he whispered in a rough voice.

"I'm not ready yet," she said.

"Oh." Sheldon stepped back, breathing heavily. Running a hand down his face, he let out a shaky laugh. "I understand."

"Thank you," Dana said quietly, though she didn't know how he could be so understanding because she herself couldn't comprehend why she couldn't move forward.

"I'm an understanding guy," Sheldon said with a rueful smile. "I better get out of here. I, ah... I'll be in touch."

"Have a good night," Dana said quietly.

She closed the door and rested her forehead against the frame. Why couldn't she freaking go forward? She'd had one-night stands in the past, so there was absolutely no reason for her to hesitate. In fact, she'd had purely sexual relationships in the past.

But she had stopped him, and deep down she knew why. Her subconscious wouldn't let her fall for this man yet, though he was darn near perfect.

Although she'd been kissing Sheldon, all she could think about was Omar.

## 10

Dana relaxed in the warm sudsy water with her eyes closed and a bath pillow at her back. A caddy secured to either side of the tub stretched across the water and contained a glass of red wine. A lit candle perfumed the air with the scent of lemons and blood orange, and her cell phone played an audiobook—the latest literary treasure bounding up the best-seller list.

Although she wasn't teaching classes this summer, she prepared for the fall by browsing bookstores and purchasing books to read before introducing them to her students. The latter part of the day she spent with teacher friends, shooting the breeze and discussing plans for the rest of the year.

After a filling dinner, this was now her relaxation time, but her phone rang and interrupted the audiobook. The screen displayed Omar's name, and her heart flipped sideways in her chest.

She touched the speaker button. "Hey, Omar. What's up?"

"I called to give you some important news. Clear your calendar for Friday night. T-Murder is putting on a charity concert at Hot Vinyl Playhouse."

Dana wrinkled her nose. "T-Murder? Mr. Cheat On His Wife? I'm not a fan."

"Come on, she forgave him and they're back together. They even had another kid."

Dana harrumphed her distaste and wiggled her toes in the water.

"He doesn't do major concerts anymore. This is something for his fans. Set aside your reservations and remember they're raising money for a good cause. Proceeds from food and beverage sales are going to the homeless."

The combination of his voice and the warm water licking her skin did something to her. She could listen to him talk for hours.

"I don't know."

"You need to keep an open mind about hip-hop."

"His music and videos are so raunchy."

"His most popular songs are, I admit... questionable... *but*, if you listen to all the tracks on his albums, he covers a wide range of topics, from politics to police brutality. Don't get caught up in the visuals."

In all honesty, Dana knew rap was an underappreciated art form, and rappers were as varied as performers in any other part of the music industry.

"Fine. I have to admit he won me over a teeny tiny bit with the hit on his last album, 'Without You.'"

"That was written about his wife. Rumor has it, the song got them back together."

"Let's hope he keeps his penis in his pants so they can stay together this time," Dana said dryly.

Omar laughed softly. "I'm staying out of their personal business. I have a complimentary ticket and can invite up to nine people to sit with me in VIP, so you can bring your girlfriends. You in?"

She thought for a moment, then replied, "I'm in. I haven't been to hear live music in a while, and it might be fun. Can Tamika and Layla bring their fiancés?"

"The more the merrier. Matter of fact, bring your new guy too, since he's so damn special."

Dana frowned at his cutting tone. "*Okay.*"

"By the way, how was your date?"

Tracing her finger down the stem of the wine glass, she replied, "We went on a night time tour of Oakland Cemetery and then went to Six Feet Under for dinner and drinks. It was nice."

"Nice? You blew me off for nice?"

"I didn't blow you off," Dana said defensively.

He actually sounded annoyed, which came as a surprise because Omar was usually pretty chill. What was going on with him?

"You do anything else?" he asked.

She considered the question, wondering if he were fishing for information on whether she'd slept with Sheldon. They never discussed those topics with each other—at least not in detail. She saved the talk of her sexual exploits for her best friends, Tamika and Layla. Talking to Omar about having sex with another man didn't sit well with her, and she definitely didn't want to hear about the women he slept with. Besides, she already had a pretty good understanding of his activities and abilities from the details in past online articles.

"Nope," she replied.

*I turned him away at the door because I couldn't stop thinking about you.*

"A'ight, well... I'll see you on Friday night. Maybe we can arrange for you to have more than a nice time."

Wow, he was really salty tonight. Could he be jealous? If so, was he jealous as a friend who wanted to spend time with her, or as a man who viewed her new beau as competition?

"I appreciate it. Text me the details." Dana shifted and bumped the caddy with her knee. "Oops." Her wine glass wobbled, and she grabbed the stem to keep it from falling.

"What happened?"

"I'm in the bath and almost knocked my wine, candle, and phone into the water. That would have been a mess." She laughed at herself.

There was silence on the other line for a while, then Omar asked, "You're in the bath... right now?"

She paused at the oddly strained sound of his voice. "Yes."

"Bubble bath?"

The air evaporated from her lungs. Why was he asking her that? "Yes."

"You been in the bath the whole time we been talking?" His deep voice went lower as it filled with incredulity.

Her skin prickled, and her heart started racing. "Yes."

Omar fell silent, but she heard him breathing and stared at the flickering light of the candle, waiting for him to speak. To say *something*. The entire time, her heart thumped beneath the tightening nipples of her breasts.

"Omar?" she said tentatively.

"I'll text you as soon as I get off the phone. Good night, Dana."

"Good ni—"

He was already gone.

When the audiobook automatically came back on, Dana hit *Pause*. An odd burning sensation lay buried in her chest. Biting her lip, she closed her eyes and tried to understand what happened. Half the conversation had been strange. Something just happened between them, right? She wanted to reach for it but was terrified, because what if her feelings were one-sided? What if she imagined the tension, the awkwardness, the peculiar sound of his voice?

She and Omar had been friends for six years and crossed the line only once, but every now and again their interactions became weighted with tension and unspoken words, as if they were each waiting for the other to say—or *do*—something. Ask a question, make the first move.

Maybe those awkward moments were all in her head. She

wasn't his type. She wasn't a model or an actress. She wore flats, not heels, and slacks and blouses, not halter tops and mini-skirts.

Mr. Casanova frequently switched sexual partners and was known for having lovers who only said good things about him. Former lovers frequently described him as a gentleman and romantic, and of course there were rumors of his sexual prowess in bed. One source claimed to have passed out from the intensity of an orgasm he gave her. Another claimed he was hung like a horse with the stamina of a bull.

Whatever the truth, Omar had a reputation with the ladies, but no one said a bad word about him, and without a doubt the female population of Atlanta silently thanked his ex for cheating and setting him free. Why would any man, especially an eligible bachelor like Omar, settle for one woman when he could have dozens?

Hesitantly, Dana parted her thighs and slid a hand between her legs. Closing her eyes, she released the soft moan that climbed up her throat as her fingers encountered her hypersensitive flesh. She might not be what he wanted, but her swollen clit betrayed that *he* was exactly what she wanted.

She almost felt guilty for what she was about to do. She'd masturbated plenty of times but always resisted the urge to let Omar star in her fantasies. This time she held no such reservations. She touched herself, imagining his deep voice, his green eyes, and his sinfully sexy lips touching the slippery, hot flesh between her legs. She imagined caressing his broad, naked shoulders and having his thick thighs slide between hers right before he thrust into her.

Dana lifted a hand to her breasts and finished herself off with a small cry, trembling through the climax—gasping and moaning so loudly the sound echoed against the bathroom walls.

When she finally settled down, her tense muscles relaxed, and she slowly opened her eyes.

"Shit," she whispered on a pant.

Good as the release was, she suspected nothing could

compare to the real thing. She couldn't continue like this, longing for more and remaining unsatisfied.

She thought about Sheldon and their easy conversation. He didn't excite her like Omar did, whose six-year head start gave him an advantage, but given enough time, her feelings for Sheldon *could* grow.

Lifting her glass to her lips, she drained the remnants of wine in one gulp. Then she picked up the phone and dialed Sheldon's number to invite him to the Friday night concert.

## 11

"Wait, one more!" Tamika said, lifting her shot glass in the air. Everyone around the low table groaned. Tamika had already completed two toasts to celebrate the May first test launch of her cosmetic line in stores. She showed them photos of her visiting different stores and posing in selfies next to her products on the shelves.

Her walnut-brown skin glowed with bronzer, and she wore her short pixie brushed into a faux hawk—high on top and tight on the sides—and sat atop her fiancé's lap. Anton was more subdued than her outgoing personality, making them an interesting study in opposites, but they worked.

"Hurry up!" Dana shouted above the noise, holding up a shot of rum.

The crowd at Hot Vinyl Playhouse was loud as they waited for the main act, T-Murder to take the stage. The drinks were flowing and the animated crowd of mostly twenty- and thirty-somethings grooved to the sounds of the opening act, a cover band playing everything from rap to nineties R&B.

Dana and her friends sat in the balcony in one of two roped off sections with a great view and a dedicated waitress serving their group of eight. Next to Dana on the sofa were Layla and her fiancé Rashad. Beside them in a chair was Tamika on her fiancé's lap. Jay from Omar's foundation came with his wife, and they were seated to Dana's right, with Omar at the end.

She rode to the venue with him, and Sheldon was supposed to meet her there, but he hadn't arrived yet, and her last text went unanswered.

"Okay, damn, I'll hurry up." Tamika grinned, eyes alight with laughter. "I just want to say, work hard, believe in your dreams, and don't let anyone dull your shine!" She screamed the last part.

"Here, here!" they all hollered, and tossed back the shots.

Dana slammed her glass on the table and shivered as the smooth rum coursed down her throat. "Where's our waitress?" she asked, looking around.

"You want another drink? Long Island iced tea?" Omar asked, standing. The perfect host all night, he made sure everyone was comfortable and having a good time.

"I can wait."

"Nah, I'll go to the bar. Anybody else want a drink?"

The others shook their heads.

"One Long Island iced tea coming up," Omar said, leaving the table.

Dana met Tamika's eyes, which sparkled with mischief as she simultaneously arched an eyebrow. Dana arched hers right back, silently asking, *What?*

Tamika stood and signaled with her hands for Dana and Layla to follow. The three went to stand at the railing overlooking the crowd, which also gave them a view of the bar at the bottom right. The floor was crowded, with bistro tables lining the back and guests on their feet, a huddled mass dancing in front of the stage.

Literally two seconds after Omar pulled up to the bar, a woman approached as if she had been waiting for the opportunity all night. Dana couldn't blame her. His clothes gave him the perfect V-shape. The charcoal gray slacks emphasized his narrow waist and hips, while the white shirt—opened at the top to expose the strong column of his throat—made his chest and back appear broader. The woman batted her eyelashes at him and pouted sexily as she handed over a card, which he tucked into his pants pocket.

"Where's your new man?" Tamika asked.

"I don't know. He should have been here by now, or at least called to let me know he can't come." She didn't know if to be annoyed or worried.

"Probably a good thing he's not here. If you watch Omar any harder, you're going to bore a hole in his head."

Was she that obvious? She constantly reflected on the conversation they had while she was in the tub, and the way she made herself come from simply thinking about him.

She shot her friend a lethal glare, similar to the one she levied at students who dared lie about why they couldn't complete an assignment. "I'm not staring."

"Sure."

"I saw you," Layla interjected. She wore her long hair in a knot on her head and a sparkly red jumpsuit in the same shade of red as her lipstick.

Dana had opted for black jeans and a fuchsia tie-neck top and, of all things—gold heels on her feet. She wanted to make a good impression on Sheldon, but he wasn't here to see her effort.

"When did you see me staring at him?" Dana asked, challenging them.

"All night!" her friends said in unison.

The three of them busted out laughing.

When she stopped laughing, Dana brushed tears from the corner of her eye. "Really?"

Layla nodded. "Really. So can you please stop pretending you don't like him?"

"Hypothetically, it doesn't matter because I'm with someone now."

Tamika leaned across Layla. "But it's not serious yet, is it?"

"No, but it could be. Last time we went out, he brought up marriage."

Tamika lifted her eyebrows in surprise.

"He intends to move here permanently," Dana added.

"Because of you?" Layla asked.

"He didn't explicitly say so, but it was implied."

The three of them directed their gazes back to the bar, where two women chatted with Omar. They were definitely his type, both in heels and body-hugging dresses, revealing shapely figures.

He laughed easily, and though she couldn't hear his laughter, she imagined the sound of the deep-throated chuckle. The women wrote their numbers on a napkin, which Omar pocketed before he sauntered away with the drinks in hand.

"His behavior down there doesn't mean anything because he was checking you out a couple of times tonight," Tamika said.

Her friend meant well, but Omar collected numbers like other people collected marbles. Where would she fit into such a lifestyle?

"Guys, I'm fine. Like I always say, Omar and I are just friends."

He stopped to talk to someone below, the lights went down on the current act, and the emcee appeared and explained T-Murder would soon come on stage.

Dana's phone beeped, and she saw a message from Sheldon.

*Sheldon*: Sorry! Car trouble. Damn thing died on me on the highway and my phone was dead too. Bad fucking night. Can't make it.

She swallowed her disappointment.

*Dana*: No worries. Are you OK?

*Sheldon*: Yes. Call you tomorrow?

*Dana*: OK.

"He's not coming," she told her friends.

Tamika pouted and Layla gave her a sympathetic look.

"We don't need him to have a good time," Layla said.

They went to sit together on the sofa, and when Omar brought her drink, Dana gratefully accepted the tall glass. Omar and Jay went off to the side to talk, and Dana resigned herself to being dateless for the rest of the night.

Finally, T-Murder came out on stage, and when the beat dropped to introduce one of his biggest hits, the crowd went wild.

Tamika threw up her hands and let out a whoop. "Yasssss! You ladies want to dance?" Her shoulders shimmied as her gaze swung between Dana and Layla.

Not in the mood, Dana shook her head.

Layla jumped up and so did Tamika.

"Come on," Layla said, extending her hand to Dana.

"You two go ahead. I'll sit here and watch."

After more cajoling with the same result, they finally gave up and went back to the railing and started dancing. After a few minutes, their fiancés joined them, and Jay and his wife did too.

Omar strolled over and settled into the empty space on the sofa beside Dana. "Where's your man?"

"He's not coming. Car trouble." She took a sip of her tea.

"He's missing out." His gaze dropped to her feet, and his jaw tightened. "I like your shoes. They're sexy."

He noticed! His gaze met hers, and heat brushed Dana's cheeks and neck. Thank goodness for her dark complexion. If she were a fairer skinned woman like Layla, she would be red for sure.

"Thank you," she murmured, rubbing a sweaty palm on her thigh. "You're popular tonight."

"Me?"

"Don't be falsely modest. I saw you collecting numbers down there." Her heart hurt a little as the words left her lips.

"I'm a friendly guy," he said, all sly and slick, his voice dropping as he gave her one of his sideways glances. He set down his drink and stood up. "Come on, let's dance."

"*You* want to dance?" Dana teased, anticipation fluttering in her chest.

He chuckled and extended his hand. "I don't do this often, so enjoy it while you can."

Her feet would hate her in these heels, but she couldn't pass up an opportunity to dance with Omar.

"I intend to."

She took his hand and ignored the charge of warm tingles up her arm when his big hand enveloped hers.

He pulled her toward the velvet rope.

"You want to go downstairs?" she asked.

"Yeah. We're about to get in the thick of it."

"Won't dancing down there with me create problems? You know, because of your admirers from earlier." She lifted an eyebrow.

He bent to her ear and whispered, "I ain't worried about them, so you don't worry about them."

Lawd, this man did things to her. His mouth was so near to hers, she caught a whiff of the whiskey from his drink and clenched her teeth, fighting the urge to turn her head and get a taste of his mouth—anything to alleviate the tightening of arousal in the depths of her belly.

Omar led her by the hand down the stairs, and she followed him into the crowd around the stage. Twenty minutes into the set, they were packed in tight with everyone else, squished like sardines. With the combination of sexually explicit lyrics and Omar behind her, Dana let loose, dancing in the middle of the crowd as if she didn't have a care in the world.

T-Murder started rapping the lyrics to one of his biggest hits, "Bomb Pussy," an ode to the pleasure he received from being inside his woman and going down on her. With his dark umber skin glistening and gold chains flashing on his bare chest under the lights, he took the audience down memory lane. Almost every person in there lifted their hands in the air, moving like one unit from side to side as they shook their asses to the beat and screamed the raunchy lyrics.

Omar's fingertips trailed down the tattooed words on the back of Dana's neck, and she caught her breath as warm waves of sensation undulated over her skin. His light touch was unbearably erotic, and pretty soon they were grinding on each other, Omar's hands gripping her hips while she gyrated her bottom against his pelvis.

For the moment, she didn't care whether this was appropriate behavior. She didn't care that he was her friend, and chances were, he wasn't sleeping alone tonight. His hands on her waist and hips felt good, and she would continue to relish every single minute of his touch.

## 12

"I don't want to leave you guys!" Tamika moaned melodramatically.

She, Dana, and Layla were wrapped around each other in a group hug in the parking lot. The long night was over, and they were exhausted but had fun.

Finally, reluctantly, they let go.

"Bye," they said, waving at each other.

Rashad and Anton gave Omar some dap and then went in the direction of their own vehicles. Dana followed Omar to the Escalade, and he let her in before going around to the driver side.

"So, how was the show?" he asked as he climbed in.

"T-Murder did a good job. I had a great time." Her voice was hoarse from hollering.

"Yeah, me too," he said with a meaningful glance in her direction.

Heat curled through her chest as he turned on soft music and pulled into the line of vehicles exiting the lot.

They dirty-danced for most of T-Murder's set, but Dana wasn't sure if Omar was simply dancing because he made no comment about what occurred between them. And hell, his pocket was full of numbers.

She removed her shoes and propped her feet on the dashboard. The sounds of a jazz instrumental poured from the speakers, and she relaxed with the seat reclined. She felt high, as if buzzing off strong liquor or good weed. *Or off the contact with Omar.*

As they neared a traffic light, he turned left when he should have gone straight, which would take them in the direction of her house.

"Where are you going?" she asked. Then the Waffle House building came into view. "No, you didn't."

"Did you really think I would take you home without your late-night breakfast?"

Dana laughed. "Of course not."

Over the years, they had attended too many events together to count, acting as each other's escorts, particularly when Dana was between relationships or her best friends couldn't attend a function. When they stayed out after midnight—whether for a concert, a party, or the late night showing of a movie—they stopped at Waffle House.

Dana started the ritual, and though they didn't hang out so late very often, Omar didn't forget.

He parked the car. "Don't move. I already know what you want. Patty melt with hash browns," he said, opening the door.

"Smothered—"

"And covered," he finished, sounding offended. "I know what you like, sweetheart. I got you. Be right back."

*Sweetheart.* Her stomach twisted into knots.

As she watched him at the counter through the window, a male customer two seats over started chatting to Omar. Omar said something funny and made the man and the waitress taking his order laugh. A smile touched her lips. He never met a stranger and was always willing to talk to anyone. At the height of his popularity, no matter where he was or what he was doing, he took photos with fans and signed autographs until everyone was satisfied.

Dana's chest hurt, and she refocused her attention outside the window beside her, blinking back tears.

When would the ache go away?

Sometimes she considered ending their friendship, or at the very least cutting back on the amount of time they spent together. But how could she, when every minute they spent apart felt like days, and every day like months.

She simply must accept their current relationship and take her cues from him.

Sighing, she closed her eyes and waited for his return.

※

OMAR EXITED WAFFLE HOUSE WITH TWO PLASTIC BAGS containing their food. He picked up the T-bone dinner for himself and added scrambled eggs. When he climbed into the SUV, Dana's eyes were closed, but he guessed she wasn't sleeping, probably tired.

With a quick glance at her bare feet propped on the dashboard, he started the Escalade. He almost wished she had kept on the shoes. Those heels were sexy.

Although he was curious to meet her new guy friend, he was glad her date didn't show. His absence left a void, which Omar happily filled. He had taken a lot of liberties tonight, grinding on her fat ass and cupping her hips. He'd wished he could move his hands higher and cup her breasts. Right now, her bra was doing some heavy lifting. Under the high neckline of her blouse, her wonderfully large tits sat up on her chest like they did the night of the spades tournament.

Jeez, she'd been so fucking hot that night. He cleared his throat and shifted in the seat.

Dana swung her head in his direction. "You okay?"

"Something in my throat." He coughed for good measure and then concentrated on the road.

Dana closed her eyes and rested her head against the window, and Omar took his time driving and didn't initiate conversation to let her rest. Before long, he pulled up outside her townhouse. "We're here."

The announcement roused her and she stretched, shoving her breasts higher as she arched her back, and Omar's mouth went dry. He'd had a lot of fantasies about those breasts, like sucking on them long and hard until the nipples went taut from his warm mouth.

"You coming in?" Dana asked.

He should head home, but his greedy ass wanted more time with Dana and as usual didn't want the night to end. "Sure. I'd rather eat my food now instead of waiting until I get home when it'll be cold."

He picked up the bags of food while Dana slipped on those sexy gold heels and then climbed out of the car.

Following behind her, he teased, "You did good in your heels tonight."

"I did, didn't I? There's nothing I can't do if I put my mind to it," she joked.

"There you go," he said, eyes locked on the roll of her hips in the butt-hugging black jeans.

A car door slammed nearby, and her neighbor, Marcus stepped out of his silver Lexus in his scrubs. Every time Omar saw him, he became unreasonably annoyed and overreacted to everything he said. They should have developed a friendship since they were both from Brooklyn, but Marcus made his hackles rise.

He didn't like the way Marcus looked at Dana. The few times they ran into each other, he became consumed by a visceral urge to bare his teeth and snarl like a wild animal protecting its territory, possessive about what was his.

"Hi, doc," Dana greeted him.

"Hey, Dana. How's it going?"

Marcus was about six feet tall and dark-skinned with a full beard. When he initially moved in, the neighborhood went into a tizzy over the young, single doctor on the block. Dana told Omar at one point Marcus tried to talk to her, but she shot him down because they were neighbors. She didn't think it was a good idea to date anyone who lived in her neighborhood.

"Good. Long day?"

"Very long. I might sleep for the next twenty-four hours." He flashed his pearly whites.

Omar glared at him. *Cocky motherfu—*

Marcus nodded briefly at Omar, who made a noncommittal sound, and then the good doctor went toward his unit on the left, two doors down.

Dana opened her front door and led the way inside. She lived in a two-bedroom townhouse with a garage, located in a pet-friendly neighborhood, chosen for its proximity to work. Around here, people power-walked for exercise or cycled on their way to the office. The kitchen contained black appliances and pine cabinets and opened to a spacious living room which led to a patio beyond the sliding glass doors.

She slipped off her shoes on the way to the kitchen. "I have Coke and lemonade," she said in front of the open refrigerator.

Omar sat on the floral armchair catty-corner to the matching sofa. "Coke," he said.

"Coming right up."

Dana approached with their canned sodas, and he took one.

She opened her container of food and sighed. "We should not be eating this late. You're such a bad influence."

"Me? You're the one who started the terrible ritual of eating Waffle House whenever we stay out late."

"Why didn't you stop me instead of encouraging my behavior? Eating at this hour isn't going to affect your body, but my big ass knows better."

"Not a damn thing wrong with your ass," he said.

Dana seemed taken aback by the statement, her gaze skittering away from his before dipping into her food.

After dancing at Hot Vinyl with mostly liquor as sustenance, they wolfed down the meals in record time. Afterward, Omar sprawled in the chair, reluctant to leave Dana's company. He was always most comfortable in her company.

As he watched, she folded her right foot onto her knee and rubbed the sole.

"Your feet hurt?"

"A little bit." She winced and continued working on her foot. "I don't know how women walk in these on a regular basis."

"Why did you wear them?"

She shrugged and didn't look at him. "Trying something different."

Omar guessed she probably wore them for her new boyfriend, but the sucker never showed up. He was glad but experienced a twist of jealousy tightening his throat.

He observed her for a little longer and then went to sit beside her on the sofa. "I can help."

She looked at him as if he was crazy.

"Give me your foot." He held out his hand.

"You're seriously going to rub my feet?" She looked at him in shock.

"They don't call me Magic Hands for nothing," Omar said, wiggling his fingers.

Dana burst out laughing. "They call you Mr. Casanova. Nobody calls you Magic Hands."

"Give me your foot, woman."

Without waiting, Omar took her foot in his hands and placed it on top of his thighs.

## 13

Omar applied gentle pressure with his thumbs and slowly rubbed the top of Dana's foot before moving lower to massage the arch. Her feet were soft and her nails painted bright orange. He'd never had such an overwhelming urge to kiss a woman's feet but resisted the impulse.

Dana bit her lip and released a tiny sound of pleasure, which hit him in the gut.

Arching an eyebrow, he said, "I guess I don't have to ask how the foot rub feels."

"Real good," she confirmed in a dreamy voice, which encouraged him to continue.

Omar gripped her foot and applied pressure. "Repeat after me. 'Thank you, Magic Hands.'"

She laughed. "I'm not saying that."

"Say it or I'll stop." He stopped.

"Thank you, Magic Hands!" Dana hollered.

"Better."

He smiled at her, and she smiled back.

Omar turned his attention to her toes, gently squeezing and tugging them one by one.

Dana sipped her drink and then set it on a coaster on the table. "I have some news."

"Tell me."

"I've decided to attend the two-week writing workshop in Colorado—the one I told you about before. There's no reason why I can't go, and like you said, I should attend for me, because it's something I really want to do. I filled out the application and paid the deposit."

As far as he was concerned, she didn't need a class, but Dana was a perfectionist. He wasn't the least bit surprised she dived into writing with the same tenacity she approached her academic pursuits years ago.

He would have covered the cost for her, but for some ridiculous reason her pride never let her take money from him. Her independent streak was extremely annoying, but he understood the need to handle her own finances. She grew up in a household where money was always tight, so she was not only careful with her own spending, she never wanted to come across as if she were taking advantage of anyone else.

"You have your ticket already?"

"I didn't want to buy it until I was certain I would be attending. I received the confirmation so I'll buy my ticket in the next day or two."

Omar switched to the other foot and started at the top again. "Still good?" he asked.

"Mhmm," she replied, sounding lethargic.

Holding her foot in one hand, he pressed his fist into the sole, and she let out another involuntary sound of pleasure. Omar smiled to himself and moved his hand to behind her ankle, squeezing for several moments before rotating her foot in a circular motion. Then he slipped his hand higher under her pants leg and squeezed her calf, his movements slowed as he savored the softness of her skin. How far would she let him go?

He glanced up at her, and their gazes crashed into each other. "Still good?"

Dana swallowed and seemed incapable of speaking. Her mouth opened and closed twice, like a fish pulling in water, and then she said weakly, "Enough."

She tried to tug away her foot, but his hand tightened on her ankle. "Why?"

Maybe the drinks he consumed earlier had affected his thinking. Or maybe he simply no longer cared to fight what he wanted and needed to show Dana he was the man she should be with. Forget any others.

"Just... stop."

She yanked again, and he let go. She inched backward until her lower back wedged hard against the arm of the sofa, and she refused to look at him, but tension thickened the air.

When she finally lifted her gaze, everything he wanted to see was right there in her eyes. The wanting, the desire. But he also detected uncertainty.

Neither of them spoke. The air became heavier and thicker as the seconds ticked by, and the accumulated want, increasing for who knew how long, expanded in the room. How long had this undercurrent existed between them and been ignored? Years, probably, for him at least. But during the past few hours, the longing and hunger reached peak levels as they grinded on and touched each other at Hot Vinyl with an unusual disregard for propriety.

The next thing Omar knew, he vaulted across the space between them, and his mouth was on hers. A moan escaped her lips as he came down on top of her. No more waiting. No more seesawing back and forth as he wondered if he should make a move or not.

A soft sigh from Dana transmitted into his lips, and he reveled in the sound. Needing no further encouragement, he grabbed her plush ass and shifted them until she lay supine beneath him with his hard body between her thighs.

He explored her mouth, slipping in his tongue to claim this new territory. She tasted so good, he could hardly restrain himself from damn near eating her alive. Only because he didn't want to scare her did he dial back the aggressiveness of the kiss.

She didn't make keeping his self-control easy, though. Her hands roamed all over his chest and made the nipples on his pecs tighten in arousal. Each time his lips pressed to the corner of her mouth, she twisted her head toward him. If he kissed the left, she turned her head to the left, seeking closer contact as if she couldn't bear for him to only give a fraction of pleasure. She wanted his whole mouth and a complete kiss.

He loved the way she moaned under him, and he shoved his right hand beneath her top and encountered a lace-covered breast. Finally, the fullness of one tit filled his hand. Dana arched her neck, gasping as he played with the tight nipple through her bra, squeezing and pulling, elated he was finally not only kissing her but also experiencing the pleasure of touching her intimately.

She ran a bare foot up his calf to his thigh, and at this point they were dry humping, her arms looped around his neck while he continued to kiss as much of her exposed skin as he could reach—her cheeks, her neck, her arms.

He pushed her top higher on her belly, and she froze.

"Omar..." she said, resting her hands on his chest.

She must feel the out-of-control way his heart clamored against his ribs.

He stared down at her with unflinching determination. "Do you want me to stop?"

"I-I don't think we should do this."

"Do you want me to stop?" he ground out.

She swallowed. "No."

He rested on his forearms and stared down into her face. "You know what I did the other night when I called and you told me you were taking a bath?"

She shook her head.

He dragged his tongue across her full lower lip. "After I hung up the phone, I took my dick in my hand and rubbed one out to the thought of you naked in the warm, sudsy water."

She closed her eyes and grimaced as if the words pained her. When she opened her eyes again, they were darker, and she whispered, "I did the same thing."

Omar groaned and buried his face in her neck. "Are you wet right now?"

"I've been wet since we were dancing at Hot Vinyl."

He muttered a low curse. He had to see. He needed to touch her.

Rough, impatient hands hurriedly unbuttoned and unzipped her jeans, and he slipped his hand inside her panties. Dana gasped and her hips shot up.

He encountered the proof of her arousal. His thick fingers glided through the slick folds. Goddamn, she was definitely wet.

While he kissed his way down her body, she caressed his bald head, her touch as encouraging as the little impatient sounds she made while he moved toward his target.

He pressed his face between her legs, nuzzling her denim-clad sex. He could smell how much she wanted him, and the scent of her desire only made him harder. He was as rigid as a steel pole but had plans for them tonight. He didn't want to eat her yet. No, he'd taste her later, and he'd take his time too, savoring every morsel of engorged flesh.

For now, he wanted to tease her.

Omar dragged her pants past her hips but left her black lace panties in place. He dragged aside the crotch and inserted a finger into her slippery sex.

Dana cried out and arched her back off the sofa. He continued to play with her, kneading her swollen sex with the heel of his hand.

"I'm gonna make you come with my hand," he whispered in her ear, his voice ripe with hunger. "Then I'm gonna make you come with my mouth. Then I'm gonna make you come all over my dick."

He pushed in two fingers, rotating and plunging in and out in a rhythmic motion. Dana closed her eyes, whimpering as her head tossed restlessly from side to side. The way she felt around his fingers, tight and wet—he wanted that feeling elsewhere. Specifically, on his penis.

He slipped another finger inside her and continued the dance of advance and retreat. He wanted the buildup because when he came inside her that would make the act so much sweeter. As he played with her sex, he whispered dirty words in her ear, telling her what he'd do to her when he was finished and how many times he would make her come before the night was over.

Her breathing quickened, her lips fell apart, and she jerked erratically as she came, gripping his biceps in a talon-like hold while her body trembled and her muscles quivered around his fingers. He looked down into her face as she cried out, her face contorted into the most beautiful expression of agonized pleasure.

"That's it, baby. You're so damn pretty when you come."

He continued to work her clit with his thumb, stretching out the orgasmic tremors until she had nothing left to give. Finally, when she was spent and the thin ropes of her dreadlocks were loosened from their band and splayed across the chair cushion in sexy disarray, he eased his hand from between her thighs.

Eyes locked on hers, he inserted each finger into his mouth and licked her sweet nectar from each digit. Dana closed her eyes and shuddered as secondary tremors rocked her body.

Raising onto his knees, Omar straddled either side of her thighs and grabbed the waistband of her jeans to pulled them all the way off. He couldn't wait to get his mouth on her.

But the shrill sound of a phone ringing stopped him in his tracks.

## 14

Dana lifted onto her elbows. "That's my brother."
She used unique ring tones for family members, a practice she started to avoid speaking to her parents. Each individual sound allowed her to avoid running for the phone but also let her know when she needed to.

Wrestling with the rearrangement of her clothes, she scrambled to her feet. She could barely walk because her feet felt springy and detached from the rest of her, while her body sang from Omar's touch and ached for his full possession.

She rushed into the kitchen and pulled the phone from her purse on the kitchen bar.

"Hey, Tommy."

Her relationship with Tommy, whose real name was Thomas, had remained strong over the years. To this day, he and his twin sister, Theresa, called Dana whenever they needed help—personal or financial.

"Hello, my beautiful sister. How are you doing?"

He wanted something. "It's after one o'clock in the morning here," she said, running a hand over her face. "Why are you calling me so late?" Tommy attended school in California and was generally uncaring about the time difference.

"Reaching out to say I love you."

"You must need a lot of money," she muttered, keeping her voice low from Omar's listening ears.

Her brother let out an embarrassed laugh, and she envisioned the distress in his round face.

"What's going on?" she whispered.

She watched Omar pick up the empty containers and plastic bags from the living room and take them to the trash can.

"I'm in a bind," Tommy started slowly. "Since I wasn't going home for the summer, I found a job and been working for the past few weeks, but a few days ago my car died. The mechanic said it's the engine, and replacing it is gonna cost me... a lot."

"How much?" Dana asked, taking a seat on a bar stool to prepare for the bad news.

Tommy mumbled an unintelligible answer.

"What did you say?"

"Fifteen hundred bucks."

Her stomach plummeted, and she closed her eyes, resting her head against her hand. "How much do you need?"

"Fifteen hundred. All of it," he answered weakly.

"Tommy..."

"I have rent and utilities and groceries to buy," he said, sounding defensive. "I have a roommate, but it's expensive out here. I swear I've been really good with my money, but the car dying messed up all my plans. I asked mom and dad for help, but they said they don't have any extra money."

"Did you talk to Ray and Evan?" she asked, referring to their older brothers.

"Yeah. Ray said Leela got braces not too long ago, so he can't afford to help, and Evan said Ginnie's due soon. Work's been too sporadic at the shop so he can't give me the money and risk not having anything when the baby comes."

Which meant Dana was his last resource, and her trip to Colorado started slipping away.

Omar had returned to the sofa and was playing with his

phone. His fingers moved quickly across the screen, and her body quietly throbbed from the memory of those fingers sliding in and out of her.

"I'll send you the money," she said, lowering her voice a little more because Omar wouldn't approve of her decision.

If he found out she was going to forego her trip to help her brother, he'd give her a stern talking to and then try to give her the money.

She wasn't like the women he dated, who expected him to be a meal ticket. He casually paid their bills and purchased expensive gifts because he could afford to do so. She, on the other hand, went to extremes to make sure he didn't think she was using him in any way. As far as she was concerned, their relationship should be mutually beneficial and depended on them having trust and respect for each other. Friends didn't take advantage of friends.

"When will you send the money?" Tommy asked.

"I'll CashApp it as soon as we hang up."

He sighed with relief. "Thanks, Dana. I'll pay you back, I promise."

He never paid her back, but she never expected him to. Like a parent, she wanted the best for her brother and would always help him if she could. She couldn't have him struggling while she could afford to lessen his struggle. There was always next year for the writing retreat, but his situation was an emergency, and he needed an immediate resolution.

"Have you heard from Theresa?" Dana asked.

"Not for a few days, but last we talked she's having a blast in Hawaii."

Their sister was studying marine biology and accepted a low-level position with a company in Hawaii. Her meager earnings were just enough to cover room and board at the facility's housing where she shared an apartment with two other young women.

Dana and her brother talked for a few more minutes before she hung up the phone.

"Everything okay with Tommy?" Omar stretched an arm across the back of the sofa, the movement gaping open his white shirt and exposing his hair-sprinkled skin. Her impatient fingers had loosened those buttons and run over his muscular chest.

"He's fine." Dana sent the cash to her brother and set down the phone. "He needed someone to talk to about a problem."

Silence dragged between them.

Omar patted the spot next to him. "Come here."

She wanted to. She really, really wanted to, but sanity had returned. "We need to talk about what happened."

She stood, and he did too.

"I didn't really plan to do much talking." Omar walked slowly toward her.

"You know you're like a brother to me, right?"

He pulled up short. "A brother? I'm standing in front of you with a boner after you let me finger you until you came, and I'm supposed to believe you think of us as siblings? I'm not thinking of you as a sister right now, Dana. Trust me."

Her eyes dipped to the massive boner tenting his pants and then swiftly hiked back up to his face.

"I mean that I value our friendship a lot."

"You think I don't?"

"I care about you, Omar."

"And I care about you."

He came closer, filling up all the available space in the room without literally filling up all the available space in the room. He wreaked of sexuality, and every nerve in her body transmitted her need for him like a current running through a live wire.

"I made you a promise," he said, resting his hands on either side of her on the bar. "I promised to make you come on my mouth and on my dick, and I like to keep my promises."

This was such a bad idea. Having sex with him would change everything between them, but she ached so much, and the constant throbbing wouldn't go away. There was only one way to rid herself of the inconvenient discomfort between her legs—give in. Satisfy the dull pain haunting her days and nights for the past few years, and find out once and for all if Omar was as good as the rumors.

"I promise you'll be satisfied," he said in her ear. He sucked her earlobe.

To hell with her reservations. Everything between them would change, but she would deal with the fallout afterward. She wanted him to do everything he promised when he whispered all those dirty words to her on the sofa.

"Omar, I want—"

He never let her finish. She expelled a soft, gasping cry as his mouth came down hard on hers.

## 15

In between bruising kisses, Omar guided Dana upstairs. Along the way, clothes were discarded, leaving a trail that indicated the urgency with which they were ready to consume each other.

They stumbled into the dark bedroom, slivers of light coming through the blinds as they made their way over to the bed. Their breaths tangled together, coming in low, heavy spurts, magnified in the quiet of the dark room.

Angling his head to the right, he kissed her deeply, his tongue stroking into her mouth and setting off a five-alarm fire in the rest of her body. His firm mouth moved over hers with expert precision, and she could almost be satisfied with just kissing him, but it wasn't enough. She wanted more, and his erection teased her with more, hard and smooth like a column of marble against her soft belly.

Her hands traveled over his sculpted chest, exploring the texture of flesh beneath her splayed hands—firm muscle beneath soft skin—until he pulled her closer, and her bare breasts flattened against his chest.

Omar grabbed a handful of locs, tugging her head back so he could bite his way down the column of her throat. The scrape of his teeth made heat dance over her sensitive skin, and the pulse at the base of her neck tripled its frantic beating and battered the skin there. How could his touch be rough yet so good? She sighed with pleasure. Their bodies hadn't joined together yet, but she was already on the verge of coming apart.

Omar shifted them onto the bed, where he bent her over the mattress and pushed her legs apart so he could stand in the open space.

"You like getting spanked, Dana?" he asked, fisting a hand at her neck under her hair and holding her in place.

Vulnerable in that position, she was pinned to the bed, toes skimming the carpet, and Omar standing behind her like a sexy, powerful god.

Before she could answer, the large palm of his other hand landed on her left butt cheek. Dana stiffened as the delicious sting spread pleasure and pain along her jiggling flesh.

"Answer me. Do you like getting spanked?"

He hit her again, and she bit her lip through a moan, the fingers of her right hand curling into the bedsheets. "Yes," she whispered, bracing for another blow.

"I can't hear you." Seconds later, his hand came down again.

"Yes!" she hissed, louder this time, the word coupled with another moan.

She didn't want him to stop. Here in the bed, she didn't have to be responsible or smart or take care of anyone else. Her needs would be met, and she could give herself over to the one man she trusted more than any other—a man who knew how to take control and would surely satisfy her.

He hit her over and over again, alternating between each ass cheek. She closed her eyes, pushing back as best she could with limited mobility. His hand remained at her neck, holding her in place and forcing her to take the repeated hits.

Pushing up with her toes, she lifted into the blows, flesh stinging and clit throbbing and damp with lust. Each crack of his hand was followed by one of her cries.

Right when she was certain she would come, he removed his hand from her neck, but she couldn't move. Tears burned her eyes as a result of the combined punishment and reward she received from the spanking. Omar's hands smoothed down her back, and then she experienced the thrill of his mouth on the fullness of her ass. He squeezed each cheek together and then gently kissed away the pain.

She breathed easier but needed release.

His hard body came down on top of hers. "You okay, baby?" he asked in her ear.

"Yes," she whispered.

"Sure?"

"Yes."

"Good. 'Cause I'm not done."

They shifted on the bed so her head was against the pillows.

"You know what I want now, don't you?"

She nodded, a mess of anticipation between her thighs as she impatiently waited for him to do what he promised.

He kissed his way down her breasts, her engorged nipples tightening painfully against the moist swipes of his tongue. She smoothed her hands over his bald head, encouraging him with soft moans and the gentle arch of her back.

Omar continued his downward descent, swirling his tongue in her navel, kissing the soft curve of her belly, and sucking the joint where the top of her thighs met her hips. He laughed softly when she twisted restlessly with uninhibited eagerness, dying for him to put his mouth *there*, where he promised.

His bearded jaw rubbed the inside of her thigh, and she choked on a cry of need, her legs going wider as she fought the urge to beg.

"Damn, baby, you're so wet," he said in a ragged voice. His thumbs spread her lower lips as he groaned and dipped his head.

*Finally.* The bold caress of his tongue teased the tiny bud of nerves at the apex of her thighs, and her mind blanked.

He went to work, his mouth and tongue relentless in their

desire to give pleasure. Almost as erotic as his touch was watching his head between her thighs and listening to the smacking sound of his mouth as he devoured her with carnal enthusiasm.

She was already primed from the spanking, so it didn't take long for her to climax. She did so with a husky cry, back arching off the mattress as her clenching sex dripped feminine cum on his tongue.

Lips glistening, his mouth came down on hers in a scorching hot kiss and transmitted her own taste from his lips to hers. They kissed for what seemed like hours—their tongues climbing over each other and their hands exploring naked skin they'd been denied access to for years.

Omar finally tore his mouth away from hers and swore softly. "Be right back."

He hopped off the bed, mumbling something about a condom before he disappeared through the door. Dana took those moments to catch her breath, and when Omar returned with his pants, she readied for him to rejoin her on the bed.

He removed a condom from his wallet and ripped open the foil packet. Then he came down again, into her open arms.

"I've dreamed of this," he whispered, nudging his hardness at the entrance to her body.

"Me too," Dana whispered shakily.

He pushed forward and entered her body with one easy slide, and they moaned in unison as he bathed his sheathed erection in her wetness.

Dana's arms clenched around his neck. She absorbed the sensation of him filling her, stretching her delicate muscles as she pumped her hips and arched her back to better receive him.

"That's it, babe," he rasped. "Take it like a good girl."

His ardent, animalistic thrusting was exactly what she wanted. The bed creaked under the weight of their frantic movements, and her wails of pleasure filled the darkness. While inside of her, Omar's mouth meshed with hers in deliciously wet kisses, and each time he slid out and plunged home again, she clenched her fingers into his back.

The scent of sex and sweat filled her nostrils and made her grab a big lungful of air to better experience the buzz of the intoxicating aroma. As the tension in her body tightened, Dana marveled at how Omar was everything she dreamed of and more. Feet flat on the bed, she pushed up into his solid thrusts, control slipping away as he brought her closer to the brink of climax.

Then, with one final stroke, she came to shattering completion, and she screamed with abandon, her back bowed, toes tightly curled, and nails sinking into his rigid butt.

Omar stiffened above her and muttered a stream of f-bombs before he shuddered and collapsed on top of her. She bore his weight for several seconds, and then he rolled over and stared up at the ceiling.

"Damn," he whispered, running a hand down his face.

Dana floated back to Earth, spent, her languid limbs barely able to move in the aftermath of ecstasy.

Omar eased from the bed and slipped into the bathroom to dispose of the condom. When he returned, she thought there would be an awkward period as they processed what happened. Instead, he pulled her into his arms, and she willingly settled against his firm body.

Practically boneless, Dana rested her head on his shoulder and promptly fell asleep.

## 16

"Ask me another question," Dana said.

She wore a white terry-cloth robe, and Omar was naked under the covers after a shower where he spent an inordinate amount of time making sure her body was clean. He was so thorough she climaxed in the shower stall and collapsed against the wall.

She barely slept the night before because after the first time, she and Omar made love again, slower and gentler and with more affection—unlike the first time when they basically screwed like rabbits. She likened the first time to an attack, really—an attack on her defenses, her senses, and her body. The second time they made love.

She woke up multiple times during the night, and each time stared at his sleeping face, unable to believe he was in her bed. One thing for sure, all the rumors were true. Mr. Casanova delivered in the sack. This morning she woke up with aching nipples and the phantom sensation of his erection pressed between her thighs.

Because they slept late, Omar ordered an early lunch, consisting of chicken sandwiches and French fries, which they were now devouring on the bed. He sat with his legs stretched out in front of him and his shoulders against the tufted headboard, while she sat with her legs curled beside her, noshing on fries while they asked each other a series of questions. The questions crossed a line they never dared approach when they were strictly friends.

"Okay, I have a good one," Omar said. "If you could have a one night pass to sleep with anyone, who would you use it on?"

"Boris Kodjoe," Dana answered immediately. "I've been in love with him forever, and when he speaks German, he's so sexy." She sighed dramatically.

"I'll do my best to make sure you never meet that pretty motherfucker," Omar mumbled.

"You're mean," Dana said with a laugh. She ate a fry. "Who would you use your pass on?"

"Alexus Rackley, no question. She's gorgeous and has the kind of confident attitude I like."

"Who is she?"

"A plus-size model I discovered by accident. I follow her on Instagram." He licked his lips.

Dana pursed her lips. "You and your big girl fetish."

"Not a fetish, sweetheart, a preference. There's a difference."

The tabloids were aware of his preference. At one time, there was speculation about Dana after she attended a charity event with him, but Omar quickly addressed the situation, and his publicist was able to have the article removed.

"I'ma need you to unfollow her on Instagram."

"Negative. Your turn to ask a question."

Dana tapped her chin, trying to think of the perfect question to ask. "Oh, I have a good one. What's the freakiest thing you've ever done?"

Omar stared up at the ceiling as he thought. "I can only pick one?"

"Good grief, yes."

He laughed. "Okay, I guess it would be a threesome." He

shrugged. "I've had several threesomes but didn't always enjoy myself, and they're a lot of work."

"You poor baby, sounds like it was such a chore."

"You have no idea," he said, a hint of mild amusement around his eyes.

Dana dipped her fries in ketchup and said, "My answer is the same, but I've only been in one threesome."

"Oh yeah?" Omar's green eyes brightened, and he sat up, looking at her with newfound interest.

"With two men."

The smile on his face died. "Oh." He sat back against the headboard.

Dana cracked up. "You were okay with me being with a man and another woman, but two men is too much?"

"I'm not saying you nasty, but you nasty."

"You were with two women!" Dana pointed out.

"Very different," he said solemnly.

"No, it's not. You're a hypocrite. I'm actually surprised you haven't done worse. I thought for sure you'd tell me you'd been in an orgy."

His mouth formed an "O," as if he remembered something.

Dana gasped and her eyes widened. "You've participated in an orgy?"

"I forgot."

She stared at him, and he stared back unflinchingly.

"How do you forget an orgy?"

"I didn't really forget, but I didn't remember when you asked the question. I was in the NFL for eight years, and we did a lot of crazy stuff. We played hard on the field and off."

"Where did this orgy take place?" Dana asked, now fascinated.

"On a yacht in Miami. Wild time, let me tell you." He shook his head.

"I'm not saying you're nasty, but you're nasty," Dana said.

Omar tossed a fry at her, which she dodged with a giggle. It fell on the mattress, and she picked it up and popped it into her mouth.

"Let me be clear, the one night pass is purely hypothetical, and I'm not letting another man into our bed," Omar said.

"Since we're laying down the law, I would like you to know I feel the same, and I'm not letting another woman into our bed. So, you have to be satisfied with me."

His eyes dragged down her body in the bulky terry-cloth robe, heat darkening his eyes as he openly ogled her. She blushed, her cheeks warming under his hungry gaze.

"Not a problem. You'll have to be satisfied with me too."

"Not a problem."

Dana's phone rang, and she hopped off the bed to pick it up from the dresser.

Sheldon. *Oh boy.*

She hesitated for a moment and then answered. "Hello?"

"Hi, Dana. Man, I'm so sorry I stood you up last night. What are you doing today? Can we get together later, and I'll make it up to you?"

Dana turned her back to Omar so she'd have a modicum of privacy. "Actually, I'm kind of busy today. I'm having lunch right now and then I'm going to a bridal boutique to help a friend choose a wedding dress."

"Are you free tonight?"

"I have plans tonight." She and Omar were going to a movie.

"What about early tomorrow afternoon?"

There was a slight pause, and then Sheldon asked, "Is everything okay?"

"Everything is fine, but... we need to talk."

"The words 'we need to talk' are never good."

"Can you do brunch tomorrow?" she asked.

"I'm busy tomorrow. Why don't you tell me now what you need to tell me so I don't waste my time?" His voice took on a hard note.

"You sound angry."

"Yeah, I'm a little angry because it's obvious what's going on here. You're dumping me because I missed last night with your friends."

"You're wrong. I—"

"My car died. Those were circumstances outside of my control."

"I'm not mad at you for missing last night. I'm not mad at you at all." She moved over to the window, putting more distance between her and Omar. Dropping her voice, she continued, "I enjoyed our times together, but I'm seeing someone else."

"I told you I'm moving here!" Sheldon said.

"And I told you, I don't want you to base your decision on us."

He let out a bitter laugh. "So you met someone last night, when I didn't show up for the concert?"

"No. This is someone I've known for a long time and we decided to... become more than friends."

"I see. Well, good luck, Dana. I hope he treats you better than you treated me."

The line went dead.

Shocked at his anger, Dana stared at the phone.

"Was that your boyfriend?" Omar asked from the bed.

"He's not my boyfriend," Dana answered.

"Not anymore," he said.

She set down the phone and climbed into bed with him. "He didn't take our conversation too well."

"Not your problem anymore. You were honest with him."

"He was so angry. I feel kinda bad, but I didn't want to just ghost him." That conversation was one of the most awkward breakups she'd ever experienced, and they weren't even a couple in a committed relationship.

"Come here," Omar said.

Dana moved the food to the nightstand and crawled across the mattress. She settled against his shoulder and stretched her arm across his wide chest. Cuddling in bed with him felt so right, and she wished they'd been honest about their attraction to each other before and taken steps sooner to move their relationship past the friend zone.

"Don't worry about him. Positive thoughts only," Omar said, winding one of her locks around his finger. "I meant to ask you last night, when do you leave for your retreat?"

Dana tensed and hesitated before answering. "I'm not going."

"Why? Last night you told me you already paid the deposit and planned to go."

She scooted away so she could look into his eyes. "Before I tell you why, promise you won't get upset."

"No," he said, dead serious.

"Omar..."

"No, because whenever someone makes that request, the listening party definitely gets upset, and I don't want you to call me a liar when I can't control my anger. Why aren't you going to Colorado?"

She hesitated, then released a deep breath. "You know Tommy called last night."

"Yes." His eyes narrowed a fraction.

"The reason he called is because his car—"

Omar was already shaking his head.

"Listen to me explain before you go off on one of your tangents," Dana said in an exasperated voice.

A muscle in his jaw tightened. "Go ahead."

"The engine blew out of his car or something, and he needs a new engine. He has a job but didn't have the money to cover the cost. He needed help so he could continue going to work and paying his bills."

"You done justifying your explanation to me and yourself?"

"I'm not justifying anything. I'm explaining what happened."

"You're not his mother, Dana."

"He doesn't have anyone else, Omar. We've talked about this before."

"And you're supposed to set aside your dreams for him?"

Swooping her hair over one shoulder, Dana said, "I'm still going to Colorado, but not this year. No big deal. I'll go to the writer's retreat next year."

"You're going this year," Omar said decisively, folding his arms over his chest.

"I'm not taking any money from you."

"It's an early Christmas gift," he said.

"It's too much."

"You didn't want me to help you when we were friends, and I can't help you now when we're more than friends? I can give money and gifts to everyone else, except the person who's most important to me?"

Her heart melted at his touching words. "I know people always have their hands out around you, and I don't want to be another person asking you for a favor or a handout."

"You're not!" Omar was the one to sound exasperated now. "And I'm sure the cost of the retreat won't break me." He sat up and cupped her face. "Sweetheart, you're not alone. You don't have to do everything by yourself and take care of everybody else. You don't have to be Wonder Woman or whatever you think you have to be with me."

His words made sense, but growing up, she was so used to scrimping and saving and seeing her parents struggle. For the longest time, she expected her life to be the same, the main reason why she had worked so hard to get her education. When she moved to Atlanta, made new friends, and realized she could thrive in this new environment, her whole perspective changed. But old habits die hard. Sometimes she was afraid to spend money in case of an emergency and was afraid to accept help because she didn't want to owe anyone.

"You can't keep sacrificing for your family and not do for yourself," he said.

"I know."

"Let me help you with this. Consider it a gift, because I know you really want to go on this retreat." He kissed her lips and touched his forehead to hers. "Let me do this for you. This one little thing."

He kissed her again, and her resolve weakened.

"Okay," she said reluctantly.

"Was that so hard?"

She laughed a little. "Very."

She straddled him on the bed. Resting her elbows on either side of his shoulders, she lowered her face to his and kissed him on the mouth.

"I wish we'd done this sooner," Dana said.

"Me too. Better late than never," he said huskily.

She lowered her lips to his, and he rolled her onto her back, their kisses going from gentle to heated within seconds. Dana's hands gripped his naked bottom, and she shifted her hips higher to grind against his.

Omar pushed open her robe and his lips fastened around her right nipple, and another intense round of lovemaking commenced.

## 17

The private dressing room of the upscale bridal boutique contained a white loveseat in the shape of a half circle and two cream-colored chairs on either side of it. Dana and Layla sat on the loveseat, while Tamika stood on a raised platform, turning to the left and then to the right in a gorgeous ball gown dress. Although Dana thought the design was lovely and looked great on her friend, Tamika's wrinkled nose indicated she didn't like the dress.

Again.

"What's wrong with this one?" Dana asked.

The boutique provided refreshments for their clients, and Dana sipped her sparkling apple cider and then placed the glass back on the table.

Tamika placed her hands on her hips. "It doesn't speak to me. I'm only going to get married once, and I have to find the perfect dress."

Initially, Tamika and her fiancé planned to get married right away. With her cosmetics business taking off and looking for a house, planning a wedding added to the list of things they needed to do, and since they were already living together, the urgency to get married waned. Tamika was now settled in her new business arrangement, she and Anton had a home under contract which they'd be closing on in a few weeks, and she loved Lion Mountain Vineyards after their trip to Dahlonega. The wedding plans were rolling along, but finding a dress proved to be a difficult task.

This was the third time they'd gone dress shopping, and they'd been at the bridal boutique for two hours. *Find a dress already!* Dana wanted to scream, but realistically, she didn't expect Tamika to rush her decision. Besides, Tamika's mother and sister passed away years before. Her next closest relative was a cousin who lived out of state, so Dana and Layla were the default persons to help her make this difficult decision.

Part of the problem was, Tamika couldn't decide if she wanted a traditional or nontraditional design or a white dress or one of a different color.

Tamika made eye contact with them in the mirrored wall. "When Anton sees me walking down the aisle, I want him to get overwhelmed with emotion and burst into tears."

The salesperson assigned to Tamika swept into the room. "How's everything in here, ladies?" she asked, stepping across the carpet in wide-legged pants and skinny four-inch heels.

Dana wondered how she managed in those shoes all day on her feet.

"I don't love it," Tamika admitted, crestfallen.

The salesperson circled the platform to stand in front of Tamika. She assessed her appearance with a critical eye, gaze traveling from her bare shoulders to the hem of the dress sweeping the floor.

"I have an idea." She wore her curly auburn hair pulled back from her face and tucked several loose tendrils behind each ear. "Do you mind if I bring you something a little different from what you've tried so far?"

"I don't know..." Tamika said hesitantly.

"Miss Jones, I've been doing this for seven years. Trust me. If you don't like the dress I choose, no problem, but please, keep an open mind. All right?"

"All right," Tamika said reluctantly.

"I'll be right back." The woman disappeared from the room.

Tamika studied her reflection. "I hope she doesn't bring me anything figure-hugging. I want big and bold. I want pizzazz."

"Remember she said to keep an open mind," Layla pointed out, eating a couple of cashews.

"I will," Tamika said, not sounding convinced. She swung toward Dana with narrowed eyes. "You're oddly quiet today. I expected you to bitch and complain that I'm taking too long."

"I slept with Omar," Dana blurted out.

"What?" Tamika shrieked.

Layla's mouths fell open.

"Before you say anything, this is—"

"I knew it!" Tamika said, slapping her hands together. "I knew you had the hots for him the entire time."

A smirk filtered across Layla's lips. "Well, well, well, the truth is finally out."

"You've wanted him for a while but put up barriers to resist the temptation," Tamika said matter-of-factly.

"Says who?" Dana asked.

"She's right," Layla interjected with a shrug. "Why do you think we tease you all the time? Last night it was more obvious than usual. You two are way too close for your friendship to be only about friendship."

"Women and men can be friends," Dana said.

"Sure, but not the two of you, clearly," Tamika said.

"Not the way you were dancing at Hot Vinyl," Layla added.

She'd known they'd give her a hard time, of course. They wouldn't be her friends if they didn't. "Are the two of you done? Because I have more to say."

Tamika hoisted the skirt of her dress higher and stepped off the platform. "I'm all ears."

Dana explained how they went back to her place to eat, how

his foot massage turned her on, and what happened as a result. "I'm happy, but... cautious."

"What do you mean you're cautious? Omar is fine, rich, and he gave you multiple orgasms in one night. Hello, what's the problem?" Tamika asked.

"For one, he's supposed to be my friend. What if we don't work out? Then I've lost a friend."

"You won't lose him," Layla said.

Tamika nodded her agreement.

Dana gnawed her bottom lip. On the ride over, outside the glow of spending time together, she thought long and hard about their situation. She didn't consider herself the jealous type, but women threw themselves at him all the time.

"I've lost track of the number of women he's dated over the years since Athena broke his heart, and I have to wonder, does he want to hook up with me, like he has those other women, or does he want more?"

"Are *you* looking for more?" Layla asked.

Dana sat with the question for a while, and her friends remained quiet, allowing her to run through her thoughts.

"Thirty days ago, I would've said no. I met so many duds, I'd decided to give up on men for a while. Then I met Sheldon and changed my mind. I did want more, but not with him or anyone else. I wanted a relationship with Omar. But he dates models and actresses. I'm a freaking English professor who's comfortable in oversized sweatshirts and cargo pants. I'm not his type."

"Are you sure?" Layla said. "Because you guys literally had sex, so you actually seem to be his type."

Tamika chimed in. "Personally, I think you need to stop overthinking this. You know Omar, you like him, and you definitely have chemistry."

Dana nodded. Tamika could be impulsive, but in this instance, she was probably right.

The saleswoman reentered the dressing room with a lacy dress hanging over her arm.

Uh-oh. The style was not among the ones Tamika liked.

Her friend simply stared. "What is that?"

"Remember what I said about keeping an open mind," the saleswoman said.

Tamika pursed her lips. "Okayyy."

"I'll help you into the dress, and then we'll see what you and your friends think." The redhead walked off toward the changing area, and Tamika scowled over her shoulder at her friends, telepathing her annoyance.

"Lord, please don't let her kill the saleswoman," Layla muttered.

With a quiet snicker, Dana popped a cube of cheese in her mouth and settled in to wait.

When Tamika returned, she stepped onto the platform and both Dana and Layla gaped at the stunning picture she made. Instead of the voluminous skirt of the ball gown, the saleswoman picked a mermaid design. The dress hugged the contours of Tamika's hips in lace before the almost sheer skirt flowed to the floor with a lace-trimmed hemline. In addition to the neckline of the lace bodice dipping to her waist, a lace cape covered her shoulders and added drama to an already breathtaking concept.

"She can remove the cape for the reception," the saleswoman said, and proceeded to do so, which showed off thin lace straps and left Tamika's back exposed.

"What do you think?" Tamika asked in a thick voice. Her emotion-filled eyes were shiny with tears.

Both Layla and Dana left the sofa and went to stand on either side of her.

"Anton's definitely going to cry. Heck, I want to cry," Dana laughed, wiping her wet eyes.

"You were right," Tamika said to the saleswoman.

The redhead simply smiled.

"You look amazing," Layla said, blinking back tears.

Both she and Dana hugged Tamika, pressing their cheeks to hers.

They all three stared at their reflection.

Tamika nodded with finality. "This is it. This is the one."

## 18

Dana had never gone tubing on the Chattahoochee, and as Omar pulled into the gravel lot of the tubing company, she wasn't convinced she'd made the right decision. She couldn't swim, and her doggy paddle skills were questionable at best, but Omar insisted she would enjoy the outing, so she accepted his invitation when he mentioned taking his son for the first time.

Today he drove his less conspicuous gray Honda Accord. As the three of them climbed out of the car, Prince's face lit up with excitement because on the drive over Omar let him watch a video of tubing on YouTube.

After a debate, they agreed on using closed tubes for the two-hour float down the river instead of letting their bottoms drag in the cold water. After Omar paid, a shuttle took them to the outpost where tubing company employees strapped life vests onto Dana and Prince and launched all three of them into the water on bright yellow tubes tethered to each other.

"Oooh, the water *is* cold," Dana said, dipping her feet in the frigid water.

"After a while, you won't notice. You okay, big man?" Omar tapped his son's tube, which was tied between theirs.

Prince was leaning back, staring up at the sky. He nodded with the vigorous enthusiasm of a typical child. "This is fun, Daddy."

They all wore shorts and water shoes, and Dana wore a tank and bikini top underneath. When they started down river, Omar removed his shirt and stuffed it beside him. His exposed skin reminded her of the passionate nights she spent in his arms the past couple of weeks, and when he caught her looking, she blushed but blew him a kiss.

Omar chose a morning trip in the middle of the week because the river would be less crowded. Nonetheless quite a few people floated around them—couples, families, and individuals. Along the banks were nothing but trees and bushes containing forested trails which drew hikers and nature lovers. The sun's warm rays weren't too bad at that time of the day, and Dana figured when the temperature increased later, the water would cool down the tubers.

They meandered slowly down the river, their positions changing every so often as they turned in a circle. Dana was glad they were tied together, because the people who weren't drifted apart from each other or struggled to stay close.

She, Omar, and Prince laughed, chatted, and teased each other. At one point, a speed boat zoomed by going upriver. Everyone waved, but mostly, the relaxing activity was filled with the quiet of the outdoors cut through by the sounds of people laughing and talking to each other.

"Look over there," Omar said, pointing.

A duck waddled to the edge of the water, jumped in, and headed straight for them.

"It's coming over here, Daddy," Prince said excitedly.

"We should have brought a camera," Dana said.

The duck unexpectedly jumped up on Prince's tube.

"Whoa," the little boy said, jerking away.

"Shoo." Dana tried to brush away the bird with her hands, but it was aggressive and flew at her. She screamed and dipped her head, but the tip of its flapping wing brushed the bun she had fixed her hair into.

"What the hell?" Omar said.

The duck landed in the water and then swam toward them again.

"It's coming back," Prince shrieked, but he didn't look afraid. There was a big grin on his face. He welcomed the confrontation.

The duck pecked at Omar's tube.

"Hey! Hey!" he said, flicking water at the animal.

"I don't think he wants us on the river. He's acting as if we're invading his territory, and he wants us to leave." Dana twisted around to watch the duck swim by.

"Why us?"

The duck quacked loudly as it swam toward a family of four.

"Bye, Mr. Duckie," Prince said, waving.

Dana and Omar looked over his head at each other and laughed. Something passed between them—a deeper sense of camaraderie and intimacy.

"I hope we don't see him again," Dana said.

No sooner had the words left her mouth than the duck coasted overhead, so low they all dipped their heads to avoid getting hit. He landed on the other side on dry land and stared at them.

"I think he really hates us," Omar muttered.

"Mr. Duckie hates us," Prince said.

They all busted out laughing at the angry duck, who waddled away into the bushes.

Afterward, the rest of the trip downriver was pleasantly uneventful. Dana let her fingers trail in the water, and several times she initiated a splashing contest with Omar and his son.

A group of people stood on top of a bridge spanning the river, and as they sailed underneath, they waved and the spectators waved at them as well. A little farther along, and they were finally at the end of the journey.

As the young male worker pulled them toward the bank, Prince said, "Yay! Can we go again?"

Omar chuckled. "Not today, big man. Another day, okay?"

When they disembarked, Prince moaned and pouted, and Omar lifted him into his arms. "What are you pouting about, huh? I'm gonna toss you right back in the water."

"No!" Prince shrieked, giggling.

"Yep, gonna toss you right back in since two hours wasn't enough."

Omar swung his son toward the water, and Prince shrieked louder.

"No?"

"No, Daddy," Prince said, vigorously shaking his head.

"You sure?" Omar held him at arm's length and pretended he was about to throw him in again.

"No! I'm sure."

"All right then." Omar set him down. "You hungry?"

"Yes!"

"What do you want to eat?"

"French fries!"

"French fries for the big man."

Omar patted his bottom and Prince skipped ahead of them. Omar flung an arm around Dana's neck and asked, "And what do you want to eat?"

"Where are you taking us?"

"A spot where we can get french fries, apparently. I have to do a better job of expanding my kid's palate."

"Actually, fries don't sound too bad. A nice fat burger and a chocolate shake to go along with them would hit the spot."

"Yeah?"

"Yes."

"Man, you're a cheap date."

Dana affected a British accent. "That's what I want you to think, but once I've sucked you in with my humble choices, I'll use my feminine wiles to get private-jet rides to Paris for dinner where we'll dine on foie gras, filet mignon, and only the best caviar, dah-ling."

"I knew it!"

Laughing, Dana threw her head back and Omar gazed at her as if she was the most beautiful woman he'd ever seen. His features softened, and then he planted a hard, wet kiss on her lips, as if he couldn't help himself.

The shuttle took them back to the main building, and while Omar lifted Prince from the vehicle, a teenager nearby did a double take at Omar. They retrieved their belongings from the lockers and were on their way to the parking lot when the boy approached.

"Excuse me, are you Omar Bradford, who used to play for the Falcons?"

"I am."

"It's him!" he said to his friends. "Do you mind if we take a selfie with you?"

"Nah, I don't mind."

The boy waved his friends over, and Omar handed Dana the tote bag with their belongings. Omar took the selfie with the teens, but their posing brought attention to him and kicked off fifteen minutes of having to sign autographs and take more pictures with other fans. A couple of the women became a little grabby and flirty, but Omar laughed good-naturedly and dutifully took photos with them as well.

This wasn't the first time Dana was with him when adoring fans swarmed, but this was the first time she'd done so after sleeping with him. Jealousy reared its hideous green head with a vengeance. She wanted to slap their hands from his biceps and tell them to shut the hell up when they made remarks like *I would love for you to tackle me.*

Instead, she gritted her teeth and patiently waited nearby with Prince until the last person received their autograph.

"Sorry about that," Omar said as they walked back to the car.

Prince walked between them, each of his hands holding on to one of theirs.

"No big deal. It's not as bad as it used to be."

"True."

Before he retired, he could easily get cornered for an hour or longer, but nowadays the fandom remained at a manageable level.

They climbed into the car, and Dana snapped on her seatbelt. "I can now check tubing off my list of accomplishments. I'm glad we came. It was very relaxing." Once again, Omar had expanded her horizons.

"Except for the part where a damn duck almost decapitated us," Omar said, talking low so his son couldn't hear him curse.

"Damn duck!" Prince shouted.

"Hey, boy, watch your mouth."

Dana giggled at them, stuffing down her jealous anger from earlier. "The duck did try to kill us, but that part was fun too." She placed a hand on Omar's thigh, and he lifted her fingers to his lips before starting the car.

They stopped at a diner for lunch and then spent the afternoon at Piedmont Park where they spread a blanket on the grass and Omar and Prince ran and jumped and tossed around a Nerf football.

After a while, Omar called out to Dana. "Come join us," he said.

"Yes, join us," Prince said.

"No way. I don't know the first thing about playing football," Dana said, shaking her head.

Prince ran over and took her hand. "Come play with us," he said, pulling on her.

With such an invitation, how could she refuse? She stood up and followed behind him. They split up into two teams, with her and Prince on one team against Omar.

Prince scored the most points simply because they let him. Imitating his father's cocky attitude every time he scored a touchdown, he spiked the ball and did his own version of the Falcons' Dirty Bird dance by flapping his arms like wings.

On the last play of the day, Omar flew into the end zone, and when Prince caught up, he tackled his legs. Omar tossed himself to the ground and Prince and Dana piled on top of him with a series of giggles, wrestling and punching until he handed over the ball in defeat.

Later, dinner was at a favorite barbecue spot before Omar took Dana home.

Standing at her door, he kissed her good night, reluctantly releasing her before he returned to the car.

After a shower and a cup of juice, Prince finally settled down for the night.

Omar tucked him into bed and kissed his forehead. "Have a good night, big man." Omar straightened.

"Daddy, do you love Miss Dana?"

The question took him aback. He hadn't fully examined his feelings for Dana, but kids were so perceptive. Prince probably noticed how Omar behaved around her.

"Yes, I do."

His son grinned. "I love her too. She's nice."

"She is. Go to sleep now, okay?"

Prince turned on his side and closed his eyes.

Omar gave him another kiss on the cheek and quietly left the room.

## 19

Dana busied herself making breakfast in the kitchen of Omar's condo. She whisked eggs and chopped vegetables for a frittata with the intention of having breakfast waiting for Omar and his son when they woke up.

The kitchen opened into a spacious living room with huge windows taking up most of one wall. Every type of gadget imaginable was in the kitchen—food processors, mixers, an espresso machine. She laughed to herself. Omar didn't know the first thing about cooking, but his chef used all these devices to prepare elaborate meals for him on a regular basis.

Over the past couple of weeks, she spent the night a few times. A "sleepover" was the explanation they gave Prince. During those periods, she, Omar, and Prince watched movies, made pizzas, and played games, and they became closer. She even tucked Prince in one night.

Last night Omar left his phone on the counter, and it beeped again, the second time in five minutes. Dana poured the egg mixture into a pan and ignored the notification, but then another one came through.

*Don't do it*, she told herself.

When his phone beeped a fourth time, she could no longer

ignore the sound, telling herself she would simply turn off the volume. Except, she didn't.

She should mind her own business, but instead, she clicked on the last message and almost dropped the phone at the sight of an explicit photo of a woman's genitals on the screen.

*Do you miss it?* was the text forwarded with the graphic photo.

Her eyes widened, and she scrolled upward to see the other messages with images from the same woman, showing off bare breasts and flaunting her voluptuous body in a red bikini with a beach in the background.

Dana set down the phone and went back to cooking. The photos dampened her morning high and reminded her of the risk she took by sleeping with Omar.

They didn't exactly flaunt their relationship, preferring low-key activities like going to the park, quiet dinners in a restaurant's private dining room, or simply staying in and watching movies on TV. Few people knew they were together, thereby limiting the publicity around his dating life. The height of his popularity had passed, but he was nonetheless a celebrity, which meant who he dated was news, and women would always make passes at him. This particular woman was clearly from his past and might not know about him and Dana.

She paused in the midst of putting the pan in the oven. What was there to know? She and Omar never defined their relationship. They slept together, but what were his expectations? She knew hers. She expected them to be in a monogamous relationship, so having another woman send him naked pictures was completely unacceptable.

Should she speak up or not?

Of course she needed to speak up. She wouldn't be Dana Lindstrom if she didn't.

She was almost finished with breakfast when Omar and Prince came into the kitchen.

"Smells good in here." Omar sounded cheerful and in a good mood.

He wrapped his arms around her from behind and kissed the sensitive spot behind her ear—which he did frequently nowadays. Nonetheless, she stiffened, but he didn't notice, walking over to the coffee pot and pouring himself a cup.

"Breakfast almost ready?" He added sugar, took a sip, and grunted his satisfaction.

"Yes," Dana answered.

Omar poured three glasses of orange juice and then picked up his phone to check his messages. She watched him surreptitiously and wondered what he must be thinking of such tawdry images on his screen first thing in the morning.

No reaction. No indication lewd photos filled his screen. They were probably so normal for him he was unaffected.

He must have guessed she looked at the messages because they had been read, but he didn't say a word. Instead, he acted as if nothing was amiss while the three of them ate breakfast at the table in the kitchen. With Prince present, Dana held off on asking Omar about the naked woman texts and behaved so normally she was proud of herself. She deserved a freaking Academy Award for her restraint.

After breakfast, Prince went to play in his room, and Dana placed the dirty dishes in the sink. When Omar reached for her, she pulled back.

"What's wrong?" he asked.

"Your phone was beeping on the counter earlier. I went over to turn it off, and I saw the four texts you received this morning."

His eyes narrowed a fraction before returning to their normal size. "Okay."

"That's all you're going to say? *Okay?*"

"What would you like me to say?"

"Is it normal for you to receive those kinds of pictures? How many do you have in your phone?" Dana asked.

"You mean you didn't check for others? If you're going to

invade my privacy, why do it halfway? Why not check every text I have?"

Her face flamed. "I know I didn't have any right to go through your phone, but that's irrelevant."

"I didn't ask her to send those pictures, Dana. She sent them unsolicited."

"I understand, but she's one of many. Women regularly chase after you."

"You're exaggerating," Omar said irritably.

"I'm not, and I knew this would happen," Dana muttered, crossing her arms over her chest.

"You knew what would happen?"

"Nothing." She looked away from him.

"All of a sudden you can't speak your mind? Tell me what you're thinking because I already know it's some bullshit."

Dana straightened her back. "What I think is not bullshit. You've been with a *lot* of women, and I'm supposed to believe you and I are going to work because I'm somehow different?"

He glowered at her. "Of course you're different. I care about you."

"Caring about each other does not mean getting romantically involved is a good idea."

"Well, it certainly doesn't mean it's a bad idea," he said sarcastically.

Dana's eyes narrowed. "This is real life. There are consequences for our actions. What if this—whatever we're doing—doesn't work out?"

"What makes you so sure we won't work?"

"Honestly? Let's be real, we're not compatible."

"We're not compatible. I see." Hands on his hips, he paced the floor and bounced his head up and down as if she'd said something profound.

"Why are you repeating what I said in that tone of voice?"

He scowled at her. "Say what you really think instead of using code words."

"Tell me what you think I'm thinking. Apparently, you have something going on in that head of yours because I don't like your tone."

"I'm not one of your goddamn students, so don't talk to me like him a friggin' child, okay?"

"I don't talk to my students like they're kids because they're adults, and they act like adults," Dana shot back.

Omar bit his bottom lip, a sure sign he was furious. "Fine, I'll tell you what you're thinking. I'm not good enough for you."

"What! You're wrong." She couldn't believe he said something so ridiculous.

"Am I? I don't read a lot or get the references to historical facts or authors you're always talking about like they're common knowledge. I'm definitely not a professor or scientist or something equally boring."

"First of all," Dana said, pointing a finger at him, "I have never talked down to you, and those men are not boring. I take your comment personally because I'm a professor. Second of all, you and me not being compatible has nothing to do with the profession of the men I've dated. If we're being honest, I could say something similar about you. You're always running around with models and actresses and wannabe models and actresses. The women I've seen you mess around with over the years are all the same. Don't you get tired?"

"This may come as a surprise to you, but those are the only women who approach me. So like a normal human being, I go where I'm wanted."

His response surprised her. Maybe those were the only woman bold enough to approach him, but if she did a survey of Atlanta women to find out which ones were interested, they'd come from all walks of life and the full range of socio-economic backgrounds.

"So the woman who texted you this morning, are you going there?"

"Don't be ridiculous."

"We've been sleeping together for a month, Omar. Why is this chick texting you her goddamn vagina?"

He pinched the bridge of his nose, as if her very reasonable question drained and irritated him at the same time.

"Let me repeat, I did not ask for her to text me."

"Who the hell is she?"

"I took her to the restaurant opening and haven't seen her since then."

"She clearly wants to keep seeing you." Making her voice high-pitched and syrupy, Dana added, "You're so big and strong. I would love for you to tackle me."

They stared at each other.

Finally, Omar said, "You need to grow the fuck up, Dana." He walked out of the kitchen.

She followed. "And you need to handle your women, unless there's something you need to tell me."

A pulse in his temple throbbed. "The only thing I have to say is you need to check yourself. Don't come at me talking about other women like you haven't been wildin' your damn self, and if anybody should be going through phones, it's me. I'm the one who had the cheating fiancée. So don't try to flip this on me like I'm the bad guy, when the only reason you're behaving like this is because you're looking for an excuse to run."

Neither of them spoke, and his words hung in the air, a scalding indictment in the face of all her insecurities about the prudence of their new relationship status. Finally, Dana huffed out an angry breath and marched into the bedroom. She grabbed her purse and overnight bag, and when she came back out, Omar stood in her path, arms crossed over his chest.

"What are you doing?" he asked.

"Leaving, because I don't appreciate you flipping this conversation around and turning a very valid concern into an attack against me."

"Leaving is your resolution?"

"Yes."

"Way to prove me wrong."

She dropped her gaze. "Get out of my way."

He couldn't blame her for her thoughts. Seeing the way he went through women, being with him meant playing Russian roulette with her heart, hoping she didn't wind up with a hole the size of a fist. Life was so much easier when they were only friends and the intimacies they shared didn't exacerbate her already complicated feelings about him.

Omar didn't move, standing in the way so long she wondered if he ever would. When he finally stepped aside, Dana rushed to the door and fled his condo—head bent uncharacteristically low.

## 20

The sun was going down as Omar stepped onto the balcony where his father relaxed and smoked a cigar because Dorothy didn't let him smoke in the house.

"Hey, Pop."

"Hey, son." Senior let a puff of smoke drift past his lips.

Omar sat across from his father, the argument with Dana a constant in his mind.

*We're not compatible.*

The words haunted him. He had taken rough falls on the football field, but nothing hit as hard as those words. Gut-punching him would have been kinder.

After Dana left his place yesterday, he texted Tracy and gently but firmly told her she could no longer send nudes or suggestive photos. He should probably send a text blast to all the women in his phone because Tracy was not the first time—nor did he expect her to be the last time—he received explicit texts.

Father and son sat in companionable silence for a while before Omar spoke.

"Do you have any regrets?" he asked.

"Regrets about what?" Senior asked.

"Regrets about actions you should have taken a long time ago but never had the courage to take."

His father chuckled. "Everybody has regrets like those. You thinking about something in particular? A relationship maybe?"

"Something like that."

"You pining for Athena?" his father asked gently.

Omar frowned. "Hell, no."

For some reason people thought he still harbored feelings for his ex. Maybe because they co-parented a child, they expected old feelings to remain. But his love for Athena died along with the end of their relationship, and if he were being truly honest, meeting Dana and developing feelings for her didn't help.

"I don't regret walking away from her, and I don't think of her as more than the mother of my son," Omar continued.

"Then what are you talking about?"

"I'm thinking about a specific person. Dana."

Being with her was surreal. Waking up together and sharing gentle, affectionate kisses with the scent of her perfume all over him was the highlight of his mornings.

"Oh," Senior said, the word loaded with commentary.

"I haven't said anything because she and I are keeping our relationship low-key for now, but we're seeing each other."

"I don't often hear you use the word relationship. Must be serious."

"It is—for me, anyway. For years, my thoughts about her have been more than friendly, and I finally acted on those thoughts."

"You slept with her?" His father quirked an eyebrow. Of course he would be blunt.

"Yes."

"You right, that's definitely more than friendly," Senior said with a hearty chuckle. "I've never met Dana, but your mother met her a couple of times when she stopped by the foundation and speaks very highly of her. We should have her over to the house one day."

"Maybe in a few days, after she calms down."

Omar explained about her reading the dirty texts and how they caused her to pull back. He reached out to her earlier today, but she never responded to his message.

"Real talk, she doesn't trust me, and it pisses me off. She knows me—has known me for years, but she can't get the idea of me as Mr. Casanova out of her head. I guess she sees me as always on the prowl, seducing hundreds of women a week or something, which is completely ridiculous."

Mr. Casanova. He never hated the name more than he did right now.

"Sounds like she has her heart sewn up in an airtight bag to protect it."

"You're right." Omar fell silent. "I'm sure I've been falling in love with her—or have been in love with her—for years, and I regret never making a move before. If I could do it all over again, as soon as my engagement with Athena ended, I'd start working on Dana."

"Regrets don't do us a bit of good," his father said. "They make you feel terrible. Action is the only way to improve your circumstances. Maybe you and Dana need to sit down and have a heart to heart."

"I would if she answered the phone. I left a couple of messages for her, but she hasn't responded yet."

"She'll come around. Right now, she's hurt, but you two have known each other too long to let a few angry words come between you."

His father was right. He didn't intend to give up on Dana but hated not being able to talk to her when he wanted. When they were only friends, sometimes weeks passed without contact because she was spending time with her girlfriends or he was hanging with his guy friends, but anytime he reached out she answered his call. Not now, and the loss of contact was destabilizing. Dana was his rock and had helped him through plenty of tough spots since they became friends. Next week he launched Kitchen Love, and he wanted her by his side.

She was smart, and he could talk to her candidly without judgment. She helped him sort through his ideas, and he learned to lean on her a lot over the years—probably more than he should—treating her like a partner instead of simply a friend.

She helped him pick the location for the foundation, after traipsing all over town with him and a real estate agent to look at properties, and they weighed the pros and cons together. When he told her about his idea to open a restaurant, which would double as a means to fight food insecurity, she stayed up all night with him while they performed preliminary research on the Internet.

Cole came onto the balcony and greeted Omar and Senior. With his back facing the yard, he tucked his hand into his pockets. "What are you two talking about?" he asked.

Omar took a moment to consider his answer to the question. His relationship with Cole was a little better, but not by much. About a month ago, he was in a foul mood for a few days but never told any of them what happened. Then he played golf with Omar and Senior once, but he didn't do very well, became upset, and left the grounds cursing. They were never able to convince him to return. For those reasons, their relationship remained tenuous at best, so Omar wasn't in the mood to divulge any information about his personal business to his brother.

"Nothing much," he answered, and quickly moved on with, "You've been off work for a while. When are you going back?"

"Why? You trying to get rid of me?" Cole sounded like he was joking, but Omar sometimes couldn't tell if he was or not.

"Nah, man, just wondering how you're able to take so much time off."

"I have a lot of banked leave. Use it or lose it, so I decided to use it. I'm going out for a bit." He left them on the balcony.

Senior looked at Omar and shrugged. "I don't know what's wrong with him. He's been restless since he came here. Something's definitely wrong, but he hasn't said a word to me or your mother. He's going through something, though."

"I wish he would talk to us," Omar said.

"You have as much chance of your wish coming true as having an end to poverty. Never gonna happen." Senior took a drag on his cigar and let the smoke float into the air.

Omar hoped his father was wrong and whatever was eating at his brother was resolved soon.

## 21

After receiving a stern talking to from her friends, Dana admitted the error of her ways. Wednesday was the last time she spoke to Omar—a full three days ago, and she missed him like crazy. Acting like a jealous shrew was not going to help their relationship, so she was going to surprise him by showing up at his place with his Father's Day gifts.

Gift-giving to a man who could literally buy anything he wanted was not always the easiest task, but with Omar, the thought truly counted. Since she could never buy him extravagant gifts, it forced her to think of unique or cute ideas he could appreciate, and she was especially excited about her choices this year.

She couldn't decide between two sets of father-son T-shirts and ended up buying both. One was black with silver lettering and said, *The Original*, while the child's T-shirt in the same color said, *The Remix*. The other T-shirt said *Me* while the smaller kid's shirt said *Mini-Me*. Both were too adorable to pass up. The third gift she purchased was a one-year membership to a hot sauce of the month club because of his penchant for spicy food. The first month's bottles were included in the gift-wrapped box.

She left Omar a voicemail earlier to let him know she was

stopping by with his gift a day early because a while back he told her that he, his father, his brother, and Prince were spending Father's Day together.

When she arrived at the building, she greeted the doorman and used the key card Omar gave her a while back to access the upper floor where he lived. She stepped off the elevator, almost skipping down the hall with the silver and blue wrapped box cradled in her arms.

She could hardly wait to see his expression when he opened the package. She rang the doorbell and waited.

He didn't come to the door, so she rang it again. Maybe he wasn't home, and she'd have to leave the package downstairs.

Then the door was opened and her ear to ear smile fumbled when she saw the woman standing in front of her. Dana recognized her right away from a few of Prince's special occasion photos Omar had shared.

This was Athena, Prince's mother and the woman Omar used to be engaged to. Full-figured with honey brown skin and long wavy hair—which at the moment was wrapped in a towel—she stood in the doorway, her obviously naked body covered in the same blue and white terry-cloth robe Dana used on the nights she stayed over. Athena looked at home, as if she lived there.

"Hi, can I help you?" Athena's eyes dipped to the box in Dana's arms.

"Hi, I-I'm a friend of Omar's. Is he here?"

Prince squeezed past his mother and grinned up at Dana. "Hi, Miss Dana. Are we having another sleep over?" he asked excitedly.

Dana's cheeks burned with embarrassment. "Hi, sweetie," she said. "No sleep over tonight."

Athena looked at her funny. "Dana, I've heard Omar talk about you before. I'm Athena, Prince's mother. Nice to meet you."

Extending one hand and balancing the box in the other, Dana shook hands with her.

"Come in, and I'll let Omar know you're here. He's in the back exercising, and you know how he gets when he's exercising. He's so focused, he has headphones on and is listening to music. Give me a second, and I'll get him."

Athena headed out of the room with Prince skipping along behind her. Dana watched her wide, swaying hips and tried her best not to be jealous, yet she was. Seeing Athena here was a slap in the face. She wanted to believe nothing was going on, but the woman was walking around his condo as if she lived there permanently, not to mention she was attractive and the mother of his child.

When Athena broke his heart, he turned into a lover man branded with the moniker Mr. Casanova. How easy would it be for him to fall back into the same old feelings while staying under the same roof as the woman he used to love?

The thought made her physically ill and brought to light her worst fear—her relationship with Omar could be fleeting.

He came into the living room, shirtless and wearing shorts, sweat glistening on his skin like a thin coat of Vaseline. Noise-canceling headphones hung around his neck, and as he came closer, she noted concern in his eyes. At least he recognized how his ex-fiancée traipsing through his apartment looked to her.

"I didn't know you were coming."

Dana tried to smile but couldn't quite get there. "I left you a voice mail but you must have already started working out. I thought I'd surprise you by bringing your Father's Day gift a little early. Happy Father's Day." She thrust the box at him and when he took it, she spun around and headed for the door.

She reached as far as a hand on the doorknob before Omar slammed his left hand above her head to block her from leaving.

"I know what you're thinking, and you're wrong."

She turned to face him, nose filling with the musky scent of masculine sweat. If she weren't upset, she probably would have jumped him.

"You have no idea what I'm thinking."

"Athena told me a while back she *might* come to town. She flew in last night, and I was going to tell you, but we haven't talked."

"Your ex-fiancé is staying at your condo and walking around naked in your face," Dana whispered fiercely. "Should I be worried?"

"Athena and I have been finished for three years," Omar said in a steely, low voice.

"Doesn't mean old feelings can't come back."

"That's exactly what it means, at least in this instance."

"I'm happy to hear your feelings for her are completely dead. Can I go now?"

Omar didn't answer, staring down at her in the silence. Then he said, "We'll finish talking outside."

He opened the door and ushered her into the hallway.

"Quick question, there aren't any vacancies in the hotels in Atlanta?" Dana asked.

"She's the mother of my kid and needed a place to stay."

"And I'm your... what? Girlfriend? I didn't know what to tell her. The whole situation was awkward, especially since we haven't made our new relationship status known to many people."

"Of course you're my girlfriend, and you could have told her. I couldn't leave her out in the cold when I have an extra bedroom where she can stay, and of course she wanted to be with Prince, and Prince is with me. Do you really want me to stick her in a hotel?"

"I don't *want* you to do anything, but I'm allowed to feel how I do. I'm allowed to be uncomfortable with this whole set up." Dana flicked her hand in the direction of the doorway and then marched down the hall.

"Dana."

He caught her wrist, but she hauled away her arm.

"You're being unreasonable," Omar ground out.

"Go be with your ex, Mr. Casanova, I'm fine."

His face settled into hard lines. "Don't do that. You know good and damn well the Mr. Casanova foolishness doesn't apply to me and you."

She released a high-pitched laugh. "Everything else was true about you. You are hung, you have great stamina, and you're amazing in bed. Why should I suddenly believe you won't hop from woman to woman when I've seen it myself? Have you forgotten, I've spent years watching you go through them. One night you're with A, three weeks later you're telling me about B, two days later there's a brand new one—C! I've seen you collect phone numbers like stamps, Omar, and I was there when Athena broke your heart. You were devastated."

"I was hurt and humiliated, but I wasn't devastated," he corrected.

"Semantics," she snapped. "A while back, you told me she still wants to get with you, remember? And I'm supposed to be okay with her staying in your condo? Hell no."

"What do you want me to do? Kick her out on the street?"

"You know what, Omar, I don't want you to do anything. Go play house with your ex. Carry on, as you always have because frankly, I don't think you're taking our relationship very seriously, and I will *not* be made a fool of."

The elevator opened, and she practically stomped into the cabin. Omar stood in the hallway, an expression of displeasure on his face, the last thing she saw before the doors closed.

⁂

DANA STUMBLED OUT OF BED AND FUMBLED WITH PUTTING ON her robe. Someone was leaning on the doorbell, and she intended to kill them when she opened the door.

Bleary-eyed, she shuffled down the stairs and peered through the peephole. Though the lights weren't on, she recognized the familiar shape of Omar's head and shoulders in the dark.

She unlatched and opened the door.

"I need a place to stay tonight. My girlfriend doesn't approve of me staying at my condo while my ex is there."

She leaned her shoulder against the door, her heart squeezing at the sight of him. He looked absolutely delicious in a chest-hugging T-shirt and jeans.

"Your girlfriend?"

"Yes. I'm staking my claim, in case I wasn't clear before. You're my girlfriend."

He stepped into the apartment, effectively forcing her to move backward, and closed the door. Setting down his duffel bag, he said, "We need to talk about what happened. Really talk. Not argue."

"I wasn't trying to be difficult," Dana said defensively. She spent the rest of the day wondering if she had overreacted.

"I get it. I'd act the same way if one of your exes showed up and was staying at your place. I'd probably sit outside in my car like a psycho."

She laughed, appreciating his sense of humor and relieved the anger between them had dissipated.

"I hardly slept the last few days. All I thought about was us and all the big moments over the years. How when I considered early retirement, you're the first person I called to discuss the idea with, before I even told my parents. How you stayed with me for two days straight when I caught the flu and made sure I drank plenty of fluids. How you make sure I get my physicals every year. You're more than a friend. You're my partner, and I hate you were upset. You shouldn't have to worry about exes showing up or sexy texts."

Dana swallowed the emotion clogging her throat. "If the situation was reversed, you'd have a problem with me receiving dick pics, unsolicited or not."

"Damn right. I would be pissed." Omar pulled her against his body.

She leaned into his warm strength and reveled in the comfort of his embrace. "I was scared of losing you," she whispered, which wasn't easy to admit. She preferred to think of herself as strong and resilient. Being with Omar made her feel emotional and vulnerable.

"I know, and that's my bad. Your happiness is important to me, Dana, and I never want you to feel uncomfortable or disrespected," he said in a grave voice. "I didn't want to ask Athena to stay someplace else, but I don't have to stay at the condo."

He kissed her gently, and she wrapped her arms around his neck.

"Where do you plan to stay?" Dana asked coyly.

"I was thinking I could stay here, which should keep me out of the dog house."

"It might." Dana gave him a kiss, slipping in tongue and groaning when his hands cupped her bottom.

"It's late. Let's go to bed." Omar kissed her forehead and took her hand, leading the way upstairs.

"Yes, sir," Dana said with a big grin.

## 22

Upon the advice of one of the consultants he worked with, Omar decided to do a soft opening of Kitchen Love, which would allow them to get feedback and determine if they had adequate staff and equipment to run the non-profit restaurant on a full-scale. Based on tonight's results, they could adjust for any deficiencies in time for the grand opening in a few weeks.

Invitations went out to a limited number of people, which included food bloggers, traditional media, and community leaders who could help get the word out to the demographic they wanted to serve. Instead of offering the full menu choices, Omar and his partners opted to spotlight a sampling of the dishes, including fried catfish, meatloaf made using his mother's recipe, and a few more meat and chicken dishes. Overall, he remained confident the night would go well.

Dressed in a dark gray jacket and green shirt Dana insisted he wear because the color looked good on him and brought out the green in his eyes, Omar walked through the dining room watching volunteers straighten the tables and make final adjustments to ensure a proper presentation to the public. In the back, food preppers chopped and diced to get ready for when the orders started coming in.

Prince was with a babysitter tonight, and Dana was right there beside him as he did his inspections. She looked great, with her dreadlocks hanging down to her waist, her lips a burnt red color, her nose rings, and a hot-looking black pantsuit she paired with gold and black heels. He couldn't wait to get her home and set those heels on his shoulders, but for now he needed to be patient and simply appreciated having her by his side.

Less than an hour before opening, Dana was in the kitchen and Omar was chatting with the male and female hosts in a corner of the dining room when his parents and Athena arrived, and to his surprise, Cole walked in with them.

Dorothy walked over, and as she gave Omar a hug, she whispered in a strained voice, "He wanted to come. He said he wanted to support you."

Omar glanced at his brother, standing near the entrance in a white shirt and his hands stuffed into the pockets of his dark trousers. He'd been in Atlanta almost three months now.

"Looking good, bro," Cole remarked, coming forward.

"Thanks. Glad you came."

"Of course. I would never miss another one of your great accomplishments." He flashed a disarming grin.

Omar's back stiffened. Cole spoke a little too loud, as if he'd been drinking. Wonderful. He didn't need any drama tonight of all nights.

"Is there anything we can do to help?" Athena asked, rubbing her hands together. She wore a black cocktail dress and let her long hair cascade in loose waves down her back.

"No, but I can show you all around real quick before everyone arrives."

"Great idea," his father said, sounding odd.

Something was wrong. Omar's gaze landed on his mother, and she gave him a faint smile. She appeared downright nervous, and he suspected there must've been an argument either before they left the house or on the car ride over.

"Follow me," he said.

He showed them the dining room and pointed out the little touches like the dark wood tables, which another restaurant group donated to them. Professionals had polished the hardwood floor to a shine, and on either side of the dining room, square tables accommodated two or could be pushed away from the wall and seat four. Longer tables down the middle seated six or more, which they'd use as community tables to encourage conversations among the guests. Seating strangers next to one another encouraged people to get to know each other, and he wanted the restaurant to not only be a place where people came to fill their bellies, but came to fill their social wells with conversation and good vibes.

Hanging on the wall was a photo of the Kitchen Love garden, which for now depended on volunteers. Omar had purchased nearby land to grow vegetables and herbs, which the restaurant used to prepare dishes on the menu.

Omar led the way into the kitchen, and his gaze immediately landed on Dana. Her back faced him as she and the chef chatted.

"This is the kitchen, where the magic happens," he announced.

Cole was the last one through the door. His gaze swept the room, rolling over Dana and then doubling back, a frown creasing his brow.

Omar kept his eyes on his brother as he said, "Much of the produce you see the staff prepping for the meals came from our garden. Right now, we're only using a portion of the acreage I bought. Eventually, I want to expand and turn the property into a community garden where people in the surrounding neighborhoods can come and get produce in exchange for helping to maintain it."

Dana ended her conversation and turned to face them, and

shock registered on Cole's face. A mere second later, the smile on hers died, and her eyes widened.

"Dana, what are you doing here?" Cole asked.

"I... what are *you* doing here?" She appeared perplexed as she moved toward them.

"How do you know my brother?" Omar asked.

"*What?*" Dana exclaimed. "Your *brother?*" She looked from one to the other.

"You never told me you knew Omar," Cole said.

"Would somebody please tell me how the hell the two of you know each other?" Omar asked.

"This... this is Sheldon, the guy I dated..." Dana let the words die on her lips.

*Oh damn*, Omar thought. His brother was the man Dana had dated, and he never had a clue because she never mentioned his name.

"You said your brother's name was Cole," Dana said.

"That's what we call him," Omar explained.

"You never told me your younger brother was Omar," Dana said.

"Guess why not," Cole said sourly. The time they spent together on the golf course did little to change his jealousy. "Omar and I have different fathers. My father's first name is Cole, and my middle name is Cole. Close friends and family call me Cole."

Dana knew he and his brother had different fathers because he told her the story once when he explained about their strained relationship. Cole Reevus was Dorothy's first husband, but they split after he cheated on her, and she became a young divorcee raising an infant on her own. She met Omar's father when her son was a couple of years old, and they dated for a while before marrying.

An awkward silence filled the kitchen as Omar and his brother stared at each other.

Even the chatter among the workers quietened down.

"Oh, shit." Cole clasped his hands together and brought them to his lips, hysterical laughter falling from his lips and lighting up his brown eyes. Turning his attention to Dana, he asked, "Omar is the guy, the friend you dumped me for, right?"

She glanced at Omar, uncertainty on how to answer stamped into her face.

"Let's step into the dining room," Omar said casually.

Cole would be angry when he learned the truth, not necessarily because he was in love with Dana—though Omar didn't doubt he cared about her since she certainly was a good woman—but because he would blame Omar for interfering. Yet another reason for the rift between them to widen. This would not bode well for their already brittle relationship.

"Was it him?" Cole asked Dana.

Omar's muscles quivered with tension, but he kept his voice neutral. "Let's go outside."

Taking Dana's hand, he led the way into the dining room. The host and hostess were talking and straightening up at the front of the restaurant, but the servers and bussers would be arriving soon.

"Let her answer the question," Cole snarled, stepping up to Omar. If looks could kill, Omar would be diced into bite-sized pieces.

"Cole, that's enough," Dorothy said in a distressed voice. "Tonight is very important for your brother."

"My brother, the go-getter," Cole said, his upper lip curling in distaste. "In everything you've done over the years, you've always given a thousand percent. Everything you did."

Irritated and unable to hold his tongue anymore because of his brother's veiled insults, Omar asked, "What are you doing here?"

"Omar, baby, this is your night and you don't need to get yourself upset," Dorothy whispered, touching his arm.

"No, he's right. What am I doing here? It'll probably come as no surprise to you that mom and Senior didn't want me to come.

They thought it was a bad idea, that I would somehow create a problem on your big night. Why would they think so badly of me?" Without waiting for an answer, Cole moved closer so he and Omar were practically eye to eye. "Were they worried I would see what they didn't want me to see? You took the woman I cared about away from me."

"You're being ridiculous. We didn't have a clue you and Omar were dating the same woman. You never tell us anything," Dorothy said.

"In case you didn't notice, none of us knew you and Dana dated, but a couple of dates don't make a relationship," Omar said. "Much as you hate to admit the truth, she was never yours to begin with."

Standing so close, he smelled liquor on his brother's breath, which explained the reckless energy emanating from him.

Cole smirked. "No, of course not, because the Almighty stepped in and stole her away."

In his current mood, Omar might swing on his brother. "If you came here to start shit, I'm not going to stoop to your level. Again, she was never yours, so I didn't steal her from you."

Cole's laughter grated on his nerves. "You're not the only one who can steal, you know."

Omar's eyes narrowed. "What the hell does that mean?"

Cole continued to laugh, louder this time, and sauntered away to one of the small tables. He sat, slouching in the chair, staring at Dana and his family with a negligent air.

"Honey, your guests will be here soon. Concentrate on having a good opening night, okay? Don't let your brother upset you." Dorothy patted Omar's arm and she, Senior, and Athena went to sit with Cole.

Dana took his hand in hers and squeezed. "I know you're upset right now, but your mom is right," she said in a low voice. "You have guests coming, including the media. This is a big night."

He didn't respond, but a muscle in his jaw tightened as he kept his gaze on his brother.

"Omar, you've been planning the opening of Kitchen Love for over two years. I know you're upset, but you have to smile and act normal, no matter how difficult it is. You don't have a choice."

"You have no idea how difficult acting normal will be with him here."

He snorted and shook his head, turning his back on his family. Why did he bother trying to fix his relationship with Cole? Nothing he did mattered over the years. So many times he'd tried, to the extent of funding his businesses—all failed endeavors—only to receive the same result. Blame. Rejection.

"You're right, I don't know how you feel, but I know you're hurting."

"I want this night to be over."

Dana leaned closer and gazed up at him. "How did you get through rough patches when you played football? Do the same tonight. Push through."

"Welcome to Kitchen Love!"

Omar and Dana swung toward the front of the restaurant, where the hosts greeted early arrivals. He recognized the couple —the woman was on the city council and her husband ran a nonprofit.

Omar straightened his shoulders and reminded himself of who he was. Dana was right. He'd been through rough patches before—injury, doubt, the loss of his grandmother, and a bunch of other events that sucked the enthusiasm out of playing football.

He always pulled through because he was Omar "Motherfucking" Bradford, and tonight he would do the same.

## 23

Despite the confrontation between him and his brother, the night was a success with only a few hiccups, all handled promptly by staff and volunteers.

The ice machine broke, but luckily toward the end of the night, so when two volunteers went to a nearby grocery store and bought bags of ice, they were sufficient to last until closing. The restaurant also ran out of ketchup because, Omar learned, the supplier shorted their order, and no one noticed. A quick run to the store and they were fully stocked again.

Because of his experience weeks ago at the restaurant opening he attended with Tracy, Omar overcompensated by having extra staff on hand in case they ran into problems. The extra people made sure the food came out of the kitchen hot and on time and two kitchen supervisors double checked each meal before the servers took them on the trays. They also chipped in to help with food prep when the kitchen became swamped and made sure tables were bussed and cleared off in a timely manner.

The reporters Omar spoke to asked tough but informed questions while at the same time giving him the opportunity to share the restaurant's mission in a clear and coherent way. All the diners praised the food and promised to return after the grand opening.

Athena and his family stayed until the end of the night, including Cole, whom he wished would go away. No such luck, and he watched with concern as his brother broodingly drank mixed drinks most of the night.

At the end of the evening, Omar went into the kitchen and thanked everyone for their hard work. "I really appreciate everything you did tonight. You should be proud of yourselves. We did it!" He said a few more words and then led the team in a round of applause.

Then he exited the kitchen and went back into the dining room. A few of the remaining servers were cleaning up. His parents and Athena were on their feet chatting with Dana, but Cole remained seated as if he expected another course to come from the kitchen.

His eyes followed Omar as he approached.

"Proud of you, son," Senior said, patting Omar on the shoulder.

On a natural high, Omar rubbed his hands together. "Thanks everybody. I appreciate you coming tonight and offering your moral support—"

Cole belched loudly.

Dorothy briefly closed her eyes, and Senior shook his head.

Cole slow-clapped. "Awesome job." He staggered to his feet and moved closer. "Once again, you have exceeded everyone's expectations. I kept waiting for something terrible to happen, but nothing did. Food came out on time, drinks were *great*, by the way. The bartender deserves a raise. I really have no complaints."

Fortunately, the mishaps in the kitchen stayed hidden from the front of the house, but Cole's sneering tone made the night's success sound like a failure.

"You know what, I'm in a good mood. You can't spoil my night."

"I would never dream of spoiling your night the way you spoiled my life the day you were born."

"Cole, please!" Dorothy said.

He laughed in the face of her dismay and leaned sideways to capture Dana's attention. "As soon as I saw the two of you together, I knew. You may not want to admit he's the reason you stopped seeing me, but I have experience on my side."

"Enough." Omar stepped halfway between them, partially shielding Dana from his brother's open hostility.

"All my life, Omar has been the chosen one."

"Stop it, Cole," Omar said through gritted teeth, hard pressed to resist charging at his brother.

Cole continued as if he hadn't spoken. "He's been the one to get all the preferential treatment. Started as soon as he was born. The family—the world—let him know right away he was special. Gifted. As soon as he came out of the womb, my mother stopped paying attention to me. Probably because she hated my father since he cheated on her and broke her heart. Don't get me wrong, I believe my mother loves me, but I'm pretty sure when she sees me, she sees his face.

"With Omar it's a completely different story. He's her baby boy, the star athlete. And look at the way he takes care of her." He flung his arms wide. "Bought her a house and gave her a job doing what she loves—helping people. He's a good son, right? Who wouldn't love him?"

Dana remained quiet.

"You know what's upsetting, though? No one ever wants to tell the truth. No one ever wants to *admit* he's the chosen one. Including you, Dana. I thought we understood each other because we both enjoyed history and literature and hell, the same movies. Those deep conversations, you'll never have those with him. But you know that, don't you, because you're *friends*."

"Time to go." Senior placed a restraining hand on Cole's arm, but he roughly shoved him off.

"Take your damn hands off me. You're not my father." He cut his eyes at Senior.

"I'm the man who raised you," Senior said.

"Barely," Cole spat.

Omar's fingers curled into a fist. "Either you leave now, or I carry you out," he said in a low, menacing voice.

"I'm not afraid of you, Omar. Mr. Casanova. Mr. Ladies' Man," Cole taunted with a laugh. "Mr. Casanova, when you can't even satisfy your own woman."

"If you're talking about Athena—"

"Yeah, I'm talking about Athena."

"What happened between her and me is none of your business."

"You think so?" Cole smirked. "Did you ever figure out whose boxers were in your bed?"

"Cole, no," Athena said in a low voice, a stricken expression crossing her face.

Omar's eyes swung between them, and his heart dropped. "I want all staff out of the dining room, now!" he barked.

The startled servers looked around in confusion.

"Go home. We'll finish cleaning up later."

They hustled out of the dining room, two going through the kitchen to exit out the back, leaving behind the family, Dana, and Athena.

Omar stared at his brother. His chest hurt, as if someone stomped him with steel-toed boots. "It was you?"

Cole's response was a smug, remorseless smile.

Dorothy clutched her hand to her chest. "Cole, how could you?"

He jabbed a finger at her. "You should have nothing to say to me. You always put him first. *Always*. Everything I wanted was set aside because Omar needed to go to camp. Omar needed a new uniform. Omar had an away game. What about me, huh? None of you ever thought about me." He slapped his chest. "From the day he was born, you treated me different, but once you realized he could run and throw a football, it was over. You only had one son from then on."

"Don't talk to your mother that way," Senior said.

Dorothy shook her head. "You're wrong. We loved you equally, but—"

"A damn lie and you know it. I'm not Senior's son, so I never expected him to love me the way he loved Omar, but you—you acted as if I barely existed. I'm your firstborn! But you know what, I'm good. I got my revenge, and I've been laughing my ass off for the past four years."

Omar's shoulders stiffened as the words jolted him. "Four years?"

"Yeah. Four years," Cole said meaningfully.

Their mother gasped and covered her mouth. Quiet descended on the dining room. From the corner of his eyes, Omar saw Dana's hands cover her mouth.

"Oh, god," Athena muttered, burying her face in her hands. Her shoulders hunched over as if she wanted to curl into a ball and disappear.

"What the hell are you saying, Cole?" Omar snarled, his right hand tightening into a harder fist.

"You know exactly what I'm saying."

Omar looked at Athena again, and the answer was in her eyes. Tears ran like streams down her cheeks.

"I'm sorry," she whispered brokenly.

Omar's mouth fell open and blood rushed in his ears, blocking out all sound.

The one good thing he thought came out of the relationship was a lie.

Prince wasn't his son.

Prince was Cole's son.

## 24

Omar slammed his fist into his brother's face. Dorothy hollered, and Athena screamed.

"Ohmigod!" Dana yelled.

Omar hit Cole so hard he fell backward over one of the long tables, knocking a tub of plates and glasses to the floor. The dishes smashed and broke apart with the sound of crashing cymbals.

Omar hopped over the table and jumped on top of his brother, holding him down and punching him over and over again with his right fist.

"Stop it! Stop!" Athena screamed.

Dana rushed around the table, and as Omar lifted his fist to land another blow, she grabbed his forearm. His fist swung forward with so much power, she stumbled as he almost tossed her to the floor, but she held on and kept him from landing another blow.

"Stop. You don't want to do this."

Breathing hard, fiery rage filled Omar's eyes, and he kept his brother pinned to the floor with a hand around his throat. She'd never seen him like this, and for the first few moments he clearly didn't *see* her. He'd snapped, and as she continued to hold his arm, his heavy breathing receded. He blinked rapidly to clear his vision and bring back reality.

She released his arm, and he looked down at his brother's bloodied face.

"Everything is fine. Give us a few minutes," Dana heard Omar Senior say behind her. He spoke in a calm voice as several of the staff tried to enter the dining room after they heard the commotion.

Omar came slowly to his feet as if coming out of a trance, and Cole rolled onto his side, groaning in agony. He gingerly touched his beaten face. His nose was definitely broken and his eye started to swell.

Dana led Omar over to the bar and rinsed the blood off his hand. His knuckles were red and the skin broken in multiple places. She glanced over at his mother and Athena helping Cole to his feet.

Dana retrieved the first aid kit and quietly tended to Omar's cuts. When she finished, she placed a bag of ice on his damaged hand.

Omar stared at the ice, an unreadable expression on his face. Cole had stolen the night's joy and hurt him deeply, and she didn't know what to say. She didn't know how to make him feel better.

Dorothy came over and placed a hand on his shoulder, shaking him out of his trancelike state. "We're going to take Cole to the hospital. Pumpkin, I'm so sorry. I didn't know. I..." At a loss for words, she shook her head and blinked back tears.

"You have nothing to be sorry for," Omar told her.

"From what Cole said, maybe I do. The reason you two haven't been close is clearly my fault."

"He's an asshole, excuse my language. Nothing he said excuses what he did."

She nodded but continued to look distressed.

"Go, Ma. Take him to the hospital."

"Are you going to be okay?"

"Yes. Dana's here."

Dorothy smiled briefly and then she and Athena guided Cole to the front door. On the way out, Athena looked over her shoulder at Omar, her brow wrinkled and the shame of what she'd done clear on her face.

Senior approached. "Son, I hate to leave, but—"

"It's okay, Pop. Ma needs you."

"You need me too. I'm in shock, so I know you must be." He ran a weary hand across his brow.

"I'll be fine. I need to stay and help clean up this mess and then lock up. I'll call you guys tomorrow."

"All right, well..." He hesitated, waving his hands in the air as if he didn't know what to do with them. "Dana, take care of him."

"I will," she promised.

After they left, Dana cupped his jaw. "I know it's hard right now, but you're going to be okay. You're Omar Motherfucking Bradford." She smiled at him, hoping the teasing and the memories would temporarily ease the pain.

"That's me," he said dully, and her heart broke. She couldn't begin to imagine the crushing sense of betrayal or hurt he must be suffering under, learning he'd been the victim of years of lies. His bond with Prince, whom he thought was his son—his mini-me—was now tainted.

Omar straightened his shoulders and rotated his neck. "I need to clean up this mess."

He walked out from behind the bar to survey the broken dishes on the floor.

"I'll get the broom and dustpan," Dana said.

"No, you'll sit down and rest. You've done enough tonight."

Dana rested her hands on her hips. "Last week you told me we were partners. Are we partners or not?"

He laughed, but the sound was broken and pained. "I know better than to argue with you. We're partners."

"Okay then. So as long as you're here, I'll be here. Let's get to work."

◊

Omar sat in Dana's living room with his head resting against the back of the sofa. He stared up at the ceiling, mind running a hundred miles a minute. He thought about his brother and Athena and wondered if they were still screwing around. He thought about Prince, and his heart ached.

He saw his little face when he tucked him into bed at night, his excitement when they played football together, and the way he repeated words Omar said, including dirty ones he shouldn't say at all. He'd always considered their bond unbreakable, despite his reservations when Athena first told him she was pregnant.

When he learned he was going to be a father, he'd been upset and disappointed in himself. He never envisioned himself as a father but acknowledged he had not done what was necessary to prevent getting his fiancée pregnant.

Despite his reservations, the night Prince was born, Omar took a last minute flight into New York. He arrived at the hospital minutes before he entered the world and was able to cut the umbilical cord. Once he held Prince in his arms, he was all in. Until Dana, he never believed he could love another person so much. The unveiling of tonight's secrets dealt a devastating blow to his soul.

Dana approached and handed him a cup of hot tea.

"You don't have anything stronger?" he asked.

"You don't need anything stronger," she said quietly.

"You're wrong. I would kill for a strong drink right now. A lot of strong drinks." He sipped the tea and then set the cup and saucer on the table. He didn't want it.

"Are you going to be okay?" Dana asked.

"Yeah." Then he laughed. "No, not for a very long time."

There was a moment of silence as he reflected on his relationship with Athena.

"You know what the crazy part of this whole messy situation is? I didn't want kids. When she told me she was pregnant, I was furious at myself for being so careless. I told her straight up I was getting a vasectomy because I didn't want any more kids, but I wanted a life with her. She assured me she was okay with marriage if we didn't have any more children. Then I found out she was cheating on me, but little did I know she cheated on me long before the incident around Prince's birthday."

"When you told me you and Cole didn't have the best relationship, I didn't know it was this bad. He's so angry and bitter."

"He's been angry and bitter for a long time." He brushed her bottom lip with his finger. "I'm sorry you were exposed to so much ugliness tonight. I knew he didn't like me, but I didn't have a clue how much. He doesn't just dislike me. He hates me."

Knowing how much his brother despised him hurt in a way he never expected, like a cork screw being plunged into his stomach and then twisted for good measure.

Dana took one of his hands in hers. She seemed at a loss for words, but she didn't have to talk. Her presence provided the comfort he needed. Having her by his side the entire night softened the blow of the revelation in the restaurant.

Omar pulled her under his arm, and she hugged his torso.

"At some point Athena and I need to talk," Omar said, wrapping his forefinger in one of her locs.

"Because you have to figure out what to do about Prince," Dana said.

"Yeah, and I have a million questions. The main one being, Why? I don't care so much about why she cheated with my brother, but I need to understand why she let me believe Prince was mine. For four years. Damn."

"You don't have to rush. You can take your time and figure out how you want to proceed."

He stayed quiet for a spell.

"I'm so glad you were there tonight. I don't know what would have happened if you didn't show up."

"I'll always have your back, Omar." She gazed up at him. "Like I know you'll always have mine."

"Thanks, sweetheart."

He gave her a soft kiss.

# 25

Omar and Athena sat across from each other at a table outside Alon's Bakery north of Atlanta. All around them, people ate lunch and a few pedestrians strolled the sidewalk to visit the stores in the shopping center.

Since the night of Kitchen Love's soft opening, they hadn't communicated except for a text she sent letting him know she and Prince were leaving the condo. His mother called later and told him she and his father allowed Athena and Prince to stay at the house with them until she flew back to New York.

"Thanks for meeting me," Athena said.

Omar didn't respond to the comment because he didn't agree to meet her out of the goodness of his heart. He needed an explanation for everything he'd learned a week ago, the night his life went to hell. Knowing she cheated on him three years ago had been hurtful, but finding out the man she cheated on him with was his own brother and the father of the child he thought was his, was the deepest of betrayals.

"I chose the wrong brother to have a child with."

"If you came here to sweet talk me, you're wasting your time. You slept with my brother and pretended his son was mine. The only reason I'm here is because I want to know why. Did I mistreat you in some way for you to betray me with my own brother? Were you ever going to tell me Prince wasn't mine?"

She swallowed hard and stared into her cup of coffee. Neither of them had ordered food to eat, and the coffees were more like props to give their hands something to do.

When she looked at him again, her woebegone expression almost made him feel sorry for her.

"You never did me wrong. You were a good boyfriend, and to be honest, I never really decided if I was going to tell you the truth or not. Part of me wanted to tell you, and another part of me wanted to go to my grave with the secret." She took a break to sip her coffee. "I never meant to hurt you or for any of this to happen. This is no excuse, but you and I never saw each other much when we were together. I was alone in New York, and he —Cole—was around. He helped me out with little things around the apartment every now and again. Once or twice he took me to the store and kept me company when I was missing you. Then one day he was at the apartment and... it just happened."

"Cheating is one thing, but you let me believe Prince was mine, Athena."

"I know. At first I thought he was yours, or at least *hoped* he was. He had your green eyes, so I was almost certain, but when I learned the truth, I realized he took after your mom."

"How did you find out he wasn't mine?" Omar asked.

"Cole demanded a paternity test," she replied, plucking at her napkin. "At first I denied his request, but he kept asking, and I finally agreed because I wanted to be certain. When we found out the truth, I didn't know how to tell you." She grimaced.

"So the reason you always hated taking money from me, was because of Prince's paternity."

She nodded. "Omar, I didn't want you to find out like that. I hate what Cole did. He was so... cruel."

Omar ran a hand over his bald head and watch a couple pass by. "How long were you seeing him?"

"We started messing around, and a few months later I found

out I was pregnant. I stopped sleeping with him right away. When Prince arrived, I was stressed out because you weren't around, and I felt like I was raising him on my own. Your family was great, your mom was helpful and offered advice, but Cole was there too. I don't know what prompted him to ask for the paternity test, but he did." She paused and shifted in the chair. Her voice went lower as it filled with shame and guilt. "Knowing he was the father brought us closer together for a little while, and we started messing around again. I was lonely. Then you showed up unexpectedly for Prince's birthday and found his boxers."

Omar's hand fisted on top of the table. "When I called you from the airport, he was there."

She nodded, looking everywhere but at him. "He left quickly and left behind the evidence you found. Sometimes I wonder if he did it on purpose, I don't know. After you left, I broke off the relationship, hoping you and I could work things out and get back together, but that never happened."

Omar's opinion concerning Athena and Cole didn't improve, but at least now he understood the timeline and background facts.

Tears shimmered in Athena's eyes. "I wish I could take back everything—the cheating, the lies. But if I did, then I wouldn't have my baby boy, and I love my little prince to death."

"What are you going to tell him about me and Cole? How are you going to explain this?"

She shrugged. "I don't know yet."

"We have to tell him the truth."

"I know." She sighed. "Do you know why Cole is here in Atlanta?"

"He told us he was on vacation," Omar answered.

"Not quite. He got into trouble at the management firm where he works—worked, again. This time he got one of the admins pregnant, and they're expecting a baby at the end of the summer. The owners asked him to leave, so he doesn't have a job anymore. I know all of this because I'm friends with one of the assistants working there. He's in Atlanta because he no longer has a job, and I don't think he knows what to do with himself."

Omar shook his head in disgust. As usual, his brother's private life was a mess. "He's like a big kid. I'm not surprised he's in trouble again."

They sat in silence for a while, and then Omar said, "I want to see Prince before you go back to New York."

"Any time you want to see him is fine by me. He loves you, and I want him to have a positive man like you in his life."

Her words crushed him, and he couldn't bear their emotional weight at the moment. "I need to go." Omar pushed back his chair and dropped a few bills on the table to cover the cost of the coffees.

"Omar."

He stopped, body tensing as he braced for the words.

"I'm sorry. I'm so, so sorry."

Regret filled Athena's face and clouded her eyes. He'd loved her once and planned to make a life with her. What if he had never found those boxers tangled in the sheets? He would have married her and been raising his brother's son as his own. She wanted sympathy, but all he saw was a liar and realized he'd barely escaped a life mired in deceit.

She wanted forgiveness, but he wasn't in a place to offer absolution. Maybe in time his feelings would change, but right now his only concern was for Prince. He wanted the best for him, and moving forward they—he, Athena, and Cole—needed to come to an agreement about the role he would play in Prince's life.

"I'll call you," he said, and walked away.

## 26

Dana waited outside the Atlanta airport terminal, searching for Omar's white Escalade. Within a few minutes the vehicle came toward her and slid into place beside the curb. Omar hopped out, and she ran into his arms, squealing as he lifted her off the sidewalk and then gave her a hungry kiss.

"Missed you like crazy," he murmured against her lips. "The past two weeks have been the longest of my life."

Dana blushed at his exuberant welcome. "I'm glad to be home."

"I want to hear all about your trip."

While she climbed into the passenger seat, he placed her bags in the back and then climbed into the driver's seat.

Though they talked a few times while she was away, the organizers of the writer's retreat filled their days and nights with activities, which limited the amount of outside communication she made. She filled him in, explaining how the thirty authors split into five groups of six the first week and rotated, learning different aspects of writing. The second week they implemented the tips and guidelines they learned and critiqued each other.

"Long days, hard work, but I absolutely loved it," she sighed.

"Glad to hear you enjoyed yourself."

She squeezed his thigh. If not for him, she wouldn't have been able to attend. "I learned so much and made new friends. I now have critique partners and accountability partners. With all this support, I should have a novel written by next year."

"That's what's up. My girlfriend, the author."

He was in a much better mood than when she left. He and Cole never repaired their relationship, and as far as Omar was concerned, they never would. He no longer wanted his brother in his life because Cole's animosity ran deep.

He hadn't fully adjusted to the new role of uncle, however, but at least Athena talked to Prince about the change. From what Omar told Dana, the little boy was very confused when his mother explained Omar was no longer his father. She said he took the role for a while, but now his real father, his uncle Cole, was taking over the role of father in his life. She couldn't imagine the confusion the little boy felt but figured in time he would accept the change, and they could all eventually have a normal relationship.

Both Athena and Omar assured Prince that Omar would continue to be part of his life, which Omar wanted and even Cole agreed to. Omar loved Prince deeply, and his feelings didn't change because he wasn't his biological son.

Omar took Dana to his condo, where she showered and took a nap before the welcome-home dinner Omar promised over the phone. He told her to dress up because they were going to a very nice restaurant.

"You're making such a fuss," Dana said, spritzing perfume on her wrists.

"Like I said, I missed you like crazy." Omar came up behind her and dropped a kiss to the sensitive spot behind her ear and patted her booty. She thrilled at his touch and smiled as he strutted into his large closet which doubled as a dressing room.

"Where are we going for dinner?" Dana asked.

"The restaurant at the Four Seasons," he called out. "I

booked a room there too, because I intend to get my drink on. We can spend the night and get up in the morning and have breakfast in the room."

"Nice. A little staycation, which I absolutely need after working so hard for two weeks." Dana added pins to her hair.

"I figured you would," Omar said.

She finished pinning her hair into a thick ball on top of her head and strategically placed gold hair jewelry throughout. The final touch was a pair of gold drop earrings.

When Omar came out of the dressing room, she placed her hands on her hips.

"What do you think?" She did a slow turn, giving him a 360-degree view of her curves in a black and gold wrap dress, its neckline showing off her ample bosom.

Omar's eyes lingered on the daring view of her right thigh at the split in the dress and slowly lowered to the gold heels adorning her feet. Biting his bottom lip, he shook his head.

"Damn, you look incredible, babe. Maybe we should stay in."

"Uh-uh," Dana said with a laugh, wagging her finger at him. "You promised me a nice dinner, and I'm holding you to it."

He groaned. "Fine, but let's eat fast." He gave her a quick kiss and took her hand. "Ready?"

"Ready."

They looked pretty darn good tonight, she in a new dress and Omar wearing a black shirt and black pants. When they arrived at the hotel, the valet took the Escalade and Omar took her hand in his. For them, holding hands, hugging, and kissing was the norm, an easy affection born from years of togetherness in a strong friendship.

They walked up the stairs to the second-floor restaurant where a host guided them to their table. They enjoyed a delicious three course dinner, drank most of a bottle of wine, and shared each other's dessert at the end of the meal.

Omar glanced at his phone, the second time in the last five minutes.

"Is everything okay?" Dana asked.

His gaze flicked up to her. "Yeah, yeah. I'm expecting a message from my mother, and she hasn't responded yet. I'm going to send her a quick text."

He sent the text and then leaned forward, gazing into her eyes. "You ready to go to bed?" he asked, in a low voice.

"Yes," Dana replied. "And since I've already taken a nap, I have a lot of energy."

"Lucky me."

Omar paid the bill and took her hand as they walked out of the restaurant. In the elevator with his arms around her, she leaned back into his solid chest and silently marveled at how much time she had wasted with other men, trying to find someone who made her feel as relaxed and cared for as Omar did.

They strolled out of the elevator on one of the upper floors, and as they made their way down the hall, a woman carrying large canvas bags came toward them. She glanced at Omar and gave a brief nod, then smiled at Dana as she passed.

Omar opened a door at the end of the hallway and let Dana precede him inside. The room was dark, but the curtains were open, and light from the nearby buildings cast a glow within.

"You got a suite," Dana said. She turned to face Omar.

"Only the best for you," he said, sounding solemn. He took her hand and kissed the back of her fingers. "Why don't you go into the bedroom while I get a snack from the minibar. You want anything?"

"No thanks, I'm stuffed from dinner. How do you have room for a snack?" Dana teased.

She pushed open the double doors and didn't take more than a single step before pulling up short. Candles were set up around the room along with huge bouquets of red roses and other flowers, their scent filling the air with a sweet aroma, and the entire scene giving the impression she had stepped into a candlelit garden.

More shocking than the beautiful display were the words written in red rose petals atop the white duvet on the bed.

*Will you marry me?*

Clutching a hand to her chest, Dana swung to face Omar, but her gaze dipped lower to him on one knee. A beautiful oval-cut diamond ring lay nestled in a box in his hand.

"Omar..." she breathed.

"I'm going to keep this short." He smiled. "Dana, I love you. Damn, I love you, babe. I've loved you for years and for so many reasons—your sense of humor, your kindness, and the way you always have my back. The time we spent together this summer made me realize how important you've become to me. I want to grow old with you. I want to keep whooping ass in spades, with you across the table as my partner, for the next seventy-five years. There are so many more things I want to do in life, and I want to do them all with you. Would you grant me the honor of becoming my wife... forever?"

Dana nodded vigorously. "Yes. Yes!"

Omar slipped the ring on her finger, and when he stood, he pulled her against his chest and kissed her hard on the mouth.

"I love you so much," he whispered huskily.

She gazed up at him with tear-filled eyes. "I love you too, and I can't wait to spend the rest of my life with you."

## Night and Day - a Quicksand bonus story

Newsletter subscribers, I have a treat for you! You're cordially invited to the wedding of Anton Bevins and Tamika Jones. Spend a little more time with this couple and their friends at Lion Mountain Vineyards, after a few bumps along the way, of course.

Go to this URL - BookHip.com/RAHGFWB - and download *Night and Day - a Quicksand bonus story*, which I wrote just for you. Available for a limited time. Enjoy!

## ALSO BY DELANEY DIAMOND

Enjoy other books in the Quicksand series!

### A Powerful Attraction (Quicksand #1)

Alex Barraza was only supposed to have dinner with his employee, Sherry Westbrook, but their attraction cannot be denied. They decide to keep their affair a secret, but what happens when Sherry learns the truth about him?

### Without You (Quicksand #2)

After years of cheating, Charisse finally walked away from Terrence "T-Murder" Burrell, but he wants her back. When trust is broken, can it ever be repaired?

### Never Again (Quicksand #3)

Carlos Hortado receives a second chance to be with the woman he left three years ago. But he has a secret. When Carmen finds out, will she be the one to walk away this time?

### Night and Day (Quicksand #4)

Anton doesn't know what to think of the sexy, baseball-bat-wielding firebrand who disturbed his weekend rest. But somehow he gets sucked into her charms, and after one night together, he can't get Tamika off his mind.

### What She Deserves (Quicksand #5)

Layla Fleming has changed since her breakup with Rashad Greene, and a sex-only arrangement is all she'll consider now. But will that be enough for *him*?

### The Friend Zone (Quicksand #6)

They have a great friendship, but a new man makes Omar risk their relationship to show Dana once and for all he's the only man she'll ever need.

Audiobook samples and free short stories available at www.delaneydiamond.com.

## ABOUT THE AUTHOR

Delaney Diamond is the USA Today Bestselling Author of sweet, sensual, passionate romance novels. Originally from the U.S. Virgin Islands, she now lives in Atlanta, Georgia. She reads romance novels, mysteries, thrillers, and a fair amount of nonfiction. When she's not busy reading or writing, she's in the kitchen trying out new recipes, dining at one of her favorite restaurants, or traveling to an interesting locale.

Enjoy free reads and the first chapter of all her novels on her website. Join her mailing list to get sneak peeks, notices of sale prices, and find out about new releases.

Join her mailing list
www.delaneydiamond.com

facebook.com/DelaneyDiamond
twitter.com/DelaneyDiamond
bookbub.com/authors/delaney-diamond
pinterest.com/delaneydiamond

Made in the USA
Columbia, SC
28 July 2021